Across The Caribbean

BY POTBAKE PRODUCTIONS

90 Days of Violence
Forward Ever! Backward Never!
oOh My Testicles!
Boy Days
Bend Foot Bailey

Across The Caribbean

Potbake Productions
Trincity, Trinidad and Tobago

Books may be ordered by contacting:
Potbake Productions
#3, 3rd Street West,
Beaulieu Avenue,
Trincity,
Trinidad,
West Indies
www.potbake.com
(868)640-0512
(868)487-9115

First published by Potbake Productions
ISBN: 978-976-95236-6-1

I promise to be brief. And honest. Potbake's 2009-10 Caribbean Short Story Competition is the brainchild of generosity and selfishness. In 2008 I published my first book, and whenever I'm "out there" struggling to market it along with my other releases I meet writers who claim they are "dying to get published – oh so badly! But there's simply no opportunity!" Naturally as a publisher, writer and baby entrepreneur, I reasoned that such an offering could benefit us both.

Although I promoted the competition via the Internet only, the response was fantastic. There were entries from Guyana, Barbados, St. Lucia and other dots on the map. Caribbean people living in faraway lands submitted stories. Even Europeans, Africans and South Americans entered despite their nationality. When the deadline came at the end of August we had over fifty stories.

To our disappointment more than half didn't meet the word count requirement. But that's not the interesting part. Among the remaining stories there was a rainbow of writing styles, creativity, themes and in some cases, unfortunately, the lack of these things of which I myself am sometimes also guilty.

The competition committed to publishing seventeen short stories. *The Only Man* and *Secret love* were written by the winner, Raymond Yusuf of Guyana. The other fifteen stirred the judges in one way or another. Today you have the chance to read them yourself and become a judge, for this book, perhaps the first of its kind, is an eclectic snapshot of Caribbean literature.

Lyndon Baptiste
Potbake Productions

To Caribbean people everywhere.

Foreword

I met Lyndon Baptiste three years ago when he came to the National Library and Information System Authority to ask us to purchase his book. The book entitled *90 Days of Violence* was published by Potbake Productions which I was to learn was also owned and managed by Lyndon himself. His next publication *oOh My Testicles!* whose provocative title captured the imagination of the reader was a real winner. His effective use of imagery and interspersion of dialect throughout the story immersed us in the character's world. I was so impressed with his next book, *Boys Days*, that I recommended it to the Young Adult Librarian as a possible book that the young adults could use for their reading sessions in the library. Finally we had a book written by a Trinidadian author that spoke to our youth through stories that would hold their interest from the first page to the last.

Lyndon, in his effort to harness the hopes and talents of young writers, has edited and published what we hope is the first of a series of books which showcase the work of Caribbean writers. In 2009, he came up with the idea of hosting a Caribbean short story competition to identify seventeen of the best writers from the Caribbean islands and publish their work.

The compilation of stories which make up this book depict rural life in Trinidad, Barbados, Guyana and St. Lucia, and all carry the common theme of triumph of love and the human spirit over adversity. *Tears for my mother* is a moving story in which the protagonist believes that her mother does not love her, not realising that the mother just cannot cope with the pressures of normal life anymore and what she has to do to support her family. It is not until she goes to live with her father that she learns the truth about her mother's situation and the sacrifice that she makes to raise her. The stories also capture the folklore of the Caribbean such as in *The Jumbie Boy* which tells of the story of the haunting of an area surrounding Rivulet Road Bridge in Couva, by a restless spirit which assumes the appearance of a young boy. Then other stories capture the life lessons that the older folk attempted to pass on to the younger children through the use of folktales. *Big rock soup*, which is based on Barbadian folklore, tells the story of a young man who uses a special stone to prepare a meal that unites a village by bringing out the hidden talents of its inhabitants. The winning story entitled *The Only Man* tells of the feeling of hopelessness of a middle-aged man diagnosed with prostate cancer. The writer through his language and use of imagery captures the essence of Georgetown, Guyana, and the atmosphere in the hospital.

I have attempted to give the reader, young adult and adult, a flavour of what this book is all about through brief synopses of the stories that caught my imagination. As Caribbean people, we have a rich oral tradition that is captured in these stories. Hopefully, I have done justice to the richness that abounds in the ensuing pages.

Juliet Glenn-Callender
Librarian
M.L.S., B.A.

Contents

The Only Man

He couldn't understand why such an erudite oncologist would choose to settle in such a poor, backward, unknown country. 'The salary must be absolutely none,' he thought as he stared blankly at the naked stucco walls of the waiting room. His face was serenely languid this morning, almost melancholy and his deep inset eyes lacked interest. He had lost all the zeal of a forty-five year old man. Now he sat waiting on his appointment with the doctor. He picked up an old copy of the *National Geographic* magazine and studied the picture on the cover; it was interesting, yet it was ugly to some degree. He brushed through the contents of the magazine on the cover, rest it down in its place and decided it was not fitting of him to read of such things, at least not now. Again he tapped the large, brown envelope on his leg, sighing as he waited; the agony of waiting building up in him like a piston under pressure. The content of the envelope made a scrunching sound that made him stop. He looked up to the Portuguese nurse, an awfully slender girl with exiguous fingers, activating herself on the telephone, laughing, chatting, giggling, and whenever she saw a doctor coming, she would exhort a comportment of busyness. He simply couldn't sit in the lounge and wait anymore. Moreover, watch the girl play with time so recklessly. This was too much for any one man to handle.

He got up and moved to the window; a frail finger gently resting upon his pale lips.

The nurse noticed him and with a casual smile called out to him: "He should be here any minute. Wouldn't you prefer to have a seat?"

He paid her no attention, but allowed his eyes to fall upon the jumbled building-scape of the old, clustered city. In the not so far distance, sirens wailed and horns honked continuously. He was about to ask the nurse how long he had to wait, but she cut him short.

"The doctor will see you now," she said casually, pointing to a door, while covering the speaker of the phone with one hand.

The door was labelled:

Dr. A. Nash, MD., MBBS.
Specialist in Oncology

He lent her an urbane smile and entered the cold room.

The doctor, stylishly spectacled, robed in white and stethoscoped, was sitting behind a large, glass-topped desk piled high with pastel-coloured papers and a few books here and there lending the atmosphere of a research student. He was singing the Eagle's *Hotel California* and when the words didn't come as they used to, he hummed blissfully. Behind him, a window framed a portion of the majestic coffee-coloured Demerara River with floating cargo ships that re-sembled chocolate smothered wafers. On the wall adjacent, certificates, awarded from prestigious American, British and German universities, old and new, peopled the bold blood wall.

"Please sit down," the doctor said, motioning the chair be-fore his desk.

His American accent, after twenty years, still confirmed his nationality.

"Good afternoon," he supplicated indolently.

The doctor made himself comfortable as he narrowed in on his patient.

"I was told you are the best."

Dr. Nash allowed an obsequious smile.

"We share different views," Dr. Nash, now modest, said. "What is it that troubles you?"

"I have cancer of the prostate," he said, handing the learned doctor the films in the envelope, "I have travelled the continental U.S. and all they could do was recommend some-one daring enough."

The doctor assessed the man slightly as he collected the x-rays.

"How long ago were—" the doctor asked when he cut him.

"Two weeks ago."

Nash studied the x-rays behind white light. He skipped the first two films without much interest, but by the third one, he stretched out his head, squinted his eyes, widened them and stared with disbelief, a heron scrupulously evaluating its prey. The man in the chair was indifferent. The erudite doctor had never seen such a case.

The doctor, pondering ponderously, sat down. "I have never seen anything like this."

"I know doctor. Everyone says that. I have seen some of the best men there are in the field."

"How long have—"

"Three months now," he answered the doctor.

"The tumour is metastasising quite quickly," the doctor said, his eyes forlornly intent.

"It was Professor Lake, of Columbia, who told me of you," he said.

"Lake," the doctor nodded his head, "Dr. Lake Rahm. We did research together at Columbia. You're not American are you, Mr. Ray?"

"No doctor, no, Canadian. Why are you asking?"

The doctor looked at him askance. "I feel as though I know you from somewhere. At least you have some semblance to someone" — the doctor trailed off — "but I just can't say who."

Mr. Ray laughed a weak, delicate laugh. "Perhaps we knew each other in a next life."

The doctor agreed and smiled.

"I'll want to study these films some more and take a few more."

"Good, that's good," Mr. Ray added. "I am well-off doctor, and I am willing to take all the chances there are."

Dr. Nash walked over to the window opposite him. Outside, beyond the corrugated roof of the northern wing, a garden of bright brick-red ixoras and bougainvillaea laden with white and magenta, amethyst and carrot-orange-coloured bracts colonised the fence and trellises. A black-skinned, sweaty Indian gardener was meticulously shearing a wall of needle-leaf white pines. Chartreuse brimstones butterflies fluttered prolifically from flowers to bracts. Georgetown was walking that day. In the not so far distance, half a mile, the strident cries of an ambulance pierced the nucleus of the atmosphere.

The doctor's mind for a moment was split on both the persnickety man in the flower garden and the lacklustre one in his office. Now, he felt isolated in a world of cold words, of which he *had* to choose. He didn't know how to explain the complications of such a tumour. In his lifetime, he had seen boxes of films of cancerous growths, many inexplicable, some outlandishly bizarre, and few that made his big eyes watered, but this particular one provoked the core of everything he knew on the subject of malignancy. The cancer itself seemed as though it was afflicted by a cancer of its own.

"How do you feel physically?" the doctor asked, moving away from the window to sit in his chair.

"I've had better days," the patient answered delicately to the point to which he was being nonchalant. "The pain occurs mostly during urination and often I feel a cutting pain along the pelvis."

"Hmm," the doctor agreed. "That will be. More so, you should also feel discomfort to your back and the need to urinate frequently."

"It's already happening."

"What is your response to radiation therapy?"

The frail man bowed his head as though he was jostling with a response that would signal the doctor of his pain and fatigue, both physically and emotionally.

"Not good. I'm on hormone therapy. But this, too, is useless."

"Indeed," Dr. Nash said, nodding his head as he was surprised by the patient's knowledge. "We shall have to take some more films. I will send these to Dr. Ramon Usuf, a specialist based at the Cancer Institute of America. We will seek his recommendations. How come you missed him?"

There was a spot of silence and the space between the two men seemed heavy with anxiety.

"I did not. The films were taken by him," the patient allowed his words to dangle, hyperbolising their extent. "It was he who recommended Dr. Rahm."

The doctor ate the answer with a gesture of the head and studied the films for a third time. Gently, he smacked an exiguous, well-manicured finger against his thin lips while his eyes were set in deep concentration. He picked up one of the films and returned to the x-ray light, then took up a magnifying glass and began studying the roots of the malignancy. Now, under magnification, the cancerous splotch appeared as a faultless round, clouded with blackness, density, and from it, the root strands grew out like the crisscrossing tributaries of an ancient river.

"Once he gives the green light," the doctor said, moving about agitatedly as though he was tense, "we will travel to the U.S. to operate."

"But I thought—" the impatient patient implored.

There was another long pall. Neither patient nor doctor knew what to say.

The silence broke, almost with an oddity.

"I will pay," Mr. Ray said, raising his eyes to look at the doctor. "I will pay generously."

"I will like you to understand," Dr. Nash said, now his intent was on ensuring that his patient believed him, "it's not going to be the money; it's all going to the Guyana Cancer Institute."

Again, the patient displayed the air of indifference.

"For now, leave these with me. I will study them in Oncology," Dr. Nash said, gathering the films and placing them into the large envelope.

"I want you to come by tomorrow—10:15. I'll have the x-rays taken then."

The patient stood up at the doctor's cue and the two men shook hands. It was then the doctor noticed him. How simply he was dressed—sky-blue shirt and khaki pants. His face looked dreadfully sick, emaciated. The black roots of his beard were beginning to expose more than their naked bodies, they were beginning to make him look like greying waste.

"Ten fifteen would do quite fine," the patient said and exited the office.

His head was jammed. He waited on the elevator, and couldn't tell if it were the clattering and groping of the elevator itself or if it were his brain trying to compensate him on the illness that the doctor had suggested to him. Now, he felt truly hopeless. Everything around him seemed a blur, everything moved in slow motion, even the ding of the elevator. The stainless steel doors that were stained with sweat marks and attrition drew open and a nurse with buxom breasts, thick arms and legs, and a thick face exited as he entered. Her smell was overpowering, a goatish sweat. She greeted him, this rare Whiteman in a coloured world. He didn't notice her. And she swore inaudibly as she moved down the corridor of the hospital.

Again the elevator bell dinged, but he was only aware of this when a raucous throng of commuters had rushed through the doors. He smiled level-headedly as he exited. His head was teeming with a black bag of silly thoughts that seemed like folded origami ornaments. For a moment he didn't know where he was or why he was there and had to sit down to muse over his state of being. Even this proved to be quite a task.

Now, a lone log drifting from the confluence of sanity and disease into the anonymous sea, he was thinking of everyone—his only younger brother who had died early, at the age of thirty-two, of pancreatic cancer; of his mother and father, consumed by death, one dark, rainy evening while driving home from the movies. After some time, he drew himself together and moved over to the receptionist counter. She was a pretty girl, her face covered with needless, pink, gaudy rouge and facial powder. Her thin lips, neat and moist, were neatly painted with red. He smiled down at her and asked her whether she could oblige him a piece of paper and an envelope.

She smiled and willingly she conceded.

Mr. Ray moved over to a corner of the reception counter, unburdened by the call of patients and their relatives, and slow traffic of the hospital. He set his mind on what he was writing and only raised his eyes when he was certain that he had mentioned what he truly wanted to say.

"Would you be kind enough to deliver this to Dr. Nash when time permits you?" he said nicely and offered her a hundred American dollars.

The receptionist, in pretentious modesty, refused the money. But deep down inside of her, she wanted every cent of it.

He insisted.

She conceded this time.

He thanked her.

She thanked him.

He smiled a wry, hopeless smile and walked away.

The receptionist, extremely jubilant, wasted no time in delivering the letter.

Outside, he stopped to look at the lush, tropical garden. It seemed as though it were an animated painting, for the colours, flamboyant in all senses, seemed to spring out and smother him. The gardener, resting under the shade of an adolescent royal palm, was wiping the sweat from his thick brows with the back of his big, hairy hand. The gardener noticed his unconscious stare; too often he had seen it. He walked over to him and offered him a sprig of the brick-red bougainvillea.

Inside him, his despair seemed to take on a different route. He sniffed the flowers and smelt nothing, no fragrance, no scent, no, nothing. His own body, the very one he had cared for with utter verve ceased to cooperate. The partnership deed between body and mind had liquefied.

He moved out of the compound and the heavy, clamorous cries of sirens assaulted his ears. Vehicles whizzed by, throwing the hot wind, their waste, in his face. He coughed unhealthily and his eyes watered thin tears.

Unexpectedly, there was a disastrous blaring of horns, the piercing screech of brakes, and a heavy crash.

"Oh Lawd! Haxcident!" a lawless woman screamed raucously as she raced to the dying man.

"Oh me Gawd," an African woman vending not far from the scene of the accident shouted, "he dead!"

Zealous and nosy onlookers alike rushed swiftly to the scene which was now piling into a tumult of people scurrying and hurrying. And, like army red ants that had sensed that one of their fellows was under attack, the gurney aides dashed to the sight, fighting their way into the core of the pandemonium.

"Is soocide," the African woman hollered, her face measured up with worries and fear.

"Accident!" another woman screamed.

"Is soocide," the African woman, now hysterical and truculent, shouted as she moved up hastily to the woman who screamed 'accident'.

The gardener, now at the scene, touched the patient's forehead and drew his hands over his eyes. Drops of blood ran down his nose. The gardener, saddened by the event, picked up the flower, shook his head sadly and walked away.

Dr. Nash, unaware of everything, was reading for the third time the note the receptionist had just delivered to him:

Dear Dr. Nash,

I do not think I should keep our appointment tomorrow. Everyone keeps sending me to Dr. Usuf, renowned oncologist. I must say, I simply *can't* go to him. I just cannot operate on myself. Doctor, I *am* Dr. Ramon Usuf, MD, FRCS. Thank you for your time and I deeply regret this course of mine.

Ever yours,
Dr. R. Usuf, MD.

The Jumbie Boy

John, or Johnny as his friends and family knew him, was an accountant;
well that's what they called him since he was ACCA qualified
up to level two, but he still had one more exam to sit before
he could consider calling himself that. He is a good friend of
mine; a kind and unassuming individual who would go out of
his way to help someone, that is, until his accident. You see,
Johnny was a victim of a drunken driver, who left him walking with a cane since his right leg and hip were damaged.

He held an accounting position at Caroni Limited, great at
his job, but since his accident he was a recluse, opting to
work from 7 P.M. to 2 A.M. just to avoid interacting with his
coworkers. He chose to work in the basement of the one-
hundred-year-old Sevilla House over the head office of Caroni's elite management personnel, for Johnny felt nothing but
contempt for Caroni's executives, he referred to them as 'office decorations' and since his accident he refused to even
refer to them at all. The Sevilla House is a creepy-ass building
that makes your skin crawl by just looking at it. I told him he

11

was a crazy ass to work in that building, furthermore to work nights in the damned basement.

Settling down to work one night, Johnny had no idea that this wasn't going to be his usual 'resentment-combined-with-numbers' night. Click! His ever-present Discman stopped just as the solo for *Dust in the wind* began. He tried to restart his music, but the player went dead.

I changed the batteries this morning! he thought to himself.

Just then he heard sounds coming from upstairs.

How the hell am I hearing stuff from upstairs? Through the floor and those damn thick walls?

Johnny got worried.

The noises grew louder and closer.

He knew quite well that the place was haunted, but he was never a victim of the devil's mischief. *That's why I'm downstairs; no one ever heard stuff downstairs.* He was sure no one else was in the building yet the sound of footsteps coming down the basement stairs was all Johnny could hear now. It was strange since there were only about three seconds worth of stairs and he was hearing the descending footsteps for over five minutes. His concern grew to the first stage of fright where you begin to search for a reference or some explanation to disprove what your senses are screaming at you. You try to prove that this can't be happening; not here, not now. Johnny's mind jumped to a conversation he had with Haniff, a security guard at the company. Haniff had told him a true story a caretaker of Sevilla House had once told him. Johnny then began replaying the entire thing in his mind:

"'Haniff, boy, if ah tell yuh wha happened tuh meh, you goh say dat meh arse gone chupid.'" Haniff related the caretaker's story in a cracked, old, Trinidadian accent. "'Wen d night geh cole, cole, ah does run in d big house and go down in d vault, because when dem mudda-arse and dem come out dey does want yuh real bad,'" he continued, referring to the evil spirits that no one doubted inhabited the compound. "'D vault is d only place dem nasty-smelling ting doh come, boy, like dey fraid it! One night it was so cole and den rain start tuh fall, ah say oh gosh dem ting going tuh come and try tuh make me, dem damn Jumbie and dem, ah hate them Haniff, AH HATE THEM! Wah ah mean really is ah fraid dem boy, ah really fraid dem. D Jumbie in Brechin Castle here eh like normal Jumbies nah, dem bad like crab, dem does frighten yuh till yuh cry and den dey does follow yuh home, well, almost home, till dey sure dat yuh eh coming back tah wuk again. Anyhow, as ah was tellin yuh, soon as d rain start tuh fall dat night, ah decide dat ah go run in d vault, but before I could close meh ears, ah hear a Jumbie on the side ah meh.'"

"'*Hear* you say?'" Haniff said, relaying to Johnny his question to the caretaker.

"'Yes! Ah hear him in meh head saying, 'Run yuh bitch we go ketch yuh before you reach d vault.' Well boy, ah run, jump down d stairs and speed in d vault! Ah coulda feel d Jumbie and dem on meh neck, like dey want tuh eat meh. Anyhow, ah make it tuh d vault, den hide till morning, den ah jus leave and now ah does only come back here every month-end to collec pension.'"

Bam! The door of Johnny's office slammed shut, snapping him back to reality. Notably scared after recounting the caretaker's story, he tried to calm himself. *Cool it Johnny. You might think it's a Jumbie, but remember they can't do you anything, so just cool it. Get your Discman back on and prepare the discrepancy report for the Board. Just concentrate on how much money those bastards in this company thiefing, with no regret or consequences for their actions. Yeah, get mad John, get mad!*

Clang! A chair right next to him went flying into the wall with the metal legs scraping the off-white paint that hid a hundred years of scars on the basement wall. *Say the Our Father,* he kept telling himself. But, unable to remember the prayer exactly, he tried to form his mouth into the shapes necessary to formulate the words he did remember. He merely ended up letting out little, inaudible, quirking sounds. *Ah ha!* He thought to himself, *I will run in the vault!* Slam! The two ton door of the vault slammed shut, cracking the plaster on the wall. *Shit!* Johnny started running as fast as he could, which actually were quick, hopping steps with his cane in his right hand hitting the floor in alternating taps, totally out of sync with how fast he needed it to be to keep up with his good leg. *My hip and leg in good shape,* Johnny thought to himself, not realising that his immense fear was a really good anesthetic. He ran out of the basement and straight to the exit.

"Oh relief at last!" Johnny uttered to himself, "At least I didn't fall down, like the people in those horror movies," he said with a shaky laugh.

Upon going down the four steps to the paved road outside, Johnny realised that his pace had slowed and the deafening silence he heard prior to everything going crazy had returned. *What the hell I just step into?* He was now faced with a pitch-black setting in the driveway. *What happened to the lights that were always on, even in the day? What the hell is really happening here?* Johnny didn't know what to do. He was trying to be brave, but couldn't help wonder what exactly was testing his manhood. Was it an evil force, wanting to scare the shit out of him or was it just plain evil without a purpose? Not willing to have that debate played out in his already quaking head, he hastily limped his way down the decline that commenced the quarter-mile walk to the Rivulet Road exit.

Instantly, Johnny regretted obeying his therapist and walking to and from work every day to exercise his leg and that idiotic decision to work nights, which was now haunting him, literally. He wished that he could see one of those assholes driving by, with their usual smug offers to give him a ride home. *They are never around when there's a purpose.* The pain was returning to his limbs as the struggle to keep his momentum grew increasingly difficult with each step, but as the fear gripped him, his hurting subsided to controllable levels once more.

"Why is this blasted exit so far away tonight?" Johnny questioned under his breath and, on watching the clouds of air come out his mouth, he realised it was freezing, then almost instantly, he felt a bitter, painful chill pierce his body.

The pain of the extreme cold made two things clear to Johnny; one, his body hurt like hell and two, this cold was not normal. As he neared the exit, his own, personal sanctuary, the lights that illuminated the exit, went out. It was pitch black now. The entire main road went black, as streetlight after streetlight went out as if to send a message of impending total doom to Johnny.

"So this is how it feels," Johnny stated, hoping he'd wake up from his nightmare, as one does when dreaming death is imminent and at that very moment of recognition wakes up to the reality of being home, and safe. But this was not the case for Johnny. The overwhelming feeling of being dominated by this evil had now soaked its way into his reality and his very core. *What to do?* Johnny did the only thing he could, he walked faster. The absence of light made the black surface of the street brighter than the area on either side. *What kind of darkness is this? This is evil.* It seemed to him like the light had been vacuumed out of the night, taking with it the presence of everything, but pure evil.

Johnny began feeling a spirit, or some sort of negative energy weighing on him to the point where he felt himself becoming heavier. *So this is what the old people mean when they say that 'the spirit them does come on yuh and you feel ah heaviness'.* Johnny continued walking, with his pain disappearing again. He was approaching a pleasant sight, the long white and black bridge crossing the Camden River, which ran north-south, slicing the Rivulet in half with its east-west layout. He envisioned it to be his exit to this horrible situation.

The bridge grew closer.

As Johnny approached from the west, he realized that the white and black walls of the bridge were glowing. His heart sank as he realised that his safety net had to be under the control of this malevolent spirit. Johnny stopped for a second that felt like an eternity to him to decide what to do, now only steps away from the bridge. He contemplated his own death, feeling as if this Jumbie wanted to take his soul to hell and not just frighten him. To say he was scared stiff was an understatement; Johnny couldn't move. At that moment, he felt a concentrated presence of evil to his left, instead of all around him, as it had been throughout the entire ordeal. He made deliberate attempts not to move his head and sneak a glance, petrified with what would await his gaze, but he couldn't stop his head from turning as if on auto-pilot. He closed his eyes as tightly as possible, retreating behind his own eyelids.

The voice of a child said, "Mister, you could walk meh across the bridge please?"

Johnny opened his eyes, thinking for a brief moment that he had dreamt the entire thing and was being jolted back to the real world with the voice of a little child.

The sight before him saturated his body with even more dread. With an outstretched right hand, stood an evil being so powerful it made the earth appear to shake under Johnny's very feet. While insisting it was a child, dressed in khaki short pants and a blue shirt, a uniform familiar to all residents of Trinidad and Tobago, indicative of a primary school pupil, it said again in a soft, fine, innocent voice:

"Mister."

Johnny stood there not knowing what to say but was certain this was not a damned school boy; not here and not now. Staring into a void where a person would have a face, Johnny saw only a fuzzy, black haze, like a small black hole on the shoulders of this little embodiment of pure evil.

"Mister, help me cross the bridge please?" the *thing* pleaded again.

Johnny, shaking with absolute fear and terror, looked directly at the apparition. "What is a school child doing here at this hour?" he asked, solely out of fear and simply to buy time to make an escape from the living nightmare into which he had been catapulted. He could not wrap his mind around the fact that this shit was happening. His question remained unanswered. The evil Jumbie Boy stared at him through no eyes, yet he felt its gaze fixed upon him. Suddenly, his body grew limp, as though he couldn't stand. Johnny sensed that this thing saw straight through him, discovering all his fears and weaknesses. He then thought that hiding away from society and wanting no part of a world filled with sarcasm and fake façades was emphatically not worth encountering evil spirits sent for his soul.

"No!" Johnny yelled, "I will not help you across the bridge."

The spirit pointed to the bridge. "But I can't pass, the coffins are blocking me."

Johnny's eyes widened. With the certainty of death ever present in his mind, he peered at the coffins appearing one by one on the bridge and then opening slowly to reveal the faces of the dead. Johnny felt his will to live being replaced by an acceptance of death. It was as if the Jumbie was sucking away his life force. With all his strength, he swung his cane at the evil; he hit nothing. However, his actions were sufficient to break the gaze of the *thing* and he began running. He ran like Ato Boldon determined not to place third once again. He jumped over each coffin in front of him and felt strength returning to his body, especially his right leg, as his mind made real his escape. In the distance, he heard the *thing* shout in a voice that sounded like men growling in the lowest, most sinister tone:

"Yuh lucky, yuh bitch, yuh lucky."

The blood-curdling sound fuelled his rocket boosters and, with his cane in the air never to hit the ground again, he scurried home without stopping or slowing down; save for his encounter with a pack of dogs that cost him pieces of his pants leg.

Upon arriving at his doorstep, Johnny stopped, turned his back to his home and faced outside, just like the old folks said, 'Turn around to face the Jumbies before you go inside. That way they can't follow you inside.'

Johnny couldn't sleep, he wasn't tired anyway. He concentrated on trying to believe that what had happened was real. "Lord Jesus, thank you for saving me."

Johnny prayed and waited for morning.

He came next door to me at first light on that Thursday morning.

"Man, Sean, you wouldn't believe what happened to me last night."

Johnny related every detail of his horrific experience and I believed every word, not because he was my best friend but because it had happened to me as well at the same bridge. I didn't tell a soul in fear that they'd say I was insane. I explained this to Johnny who was a bit angry at me for my secret but said that he was going to face this evil again and that *this time* he would get rid of it. I begged him to leave it alone and stay away from the bridge, but I knew in my heart that my attempts were futile for I could see the conviction in his eyes.

That was the last conversation I had with my best friend.

I became concerned when I didn't see him the next day, but I thought he was simply tired from work, so I left it alone. On Thursday, after two weeks of not seeing a peep from Johnny, I decided to leave my office early to catch him before he went to work. As I approached his home, I noticed the flashing lights of police cars. Just then, I saw the police come out of his house. I found out that Johnny was declared missing two weeks ago and his body was found by a passerby who reported it.

"How's that possible? I spoke to him exactly two Thursdays ago!"

"Sir that conversation had to have been on Wednesday, since his mother reported him missing on Thursday after he didn't come home that morning. You're in shock," the officer suggested. "Maybe you're mixing up your days."

The chill I instantly received raised every grain of hair on the back of my neck. I knew I definitely wasn't mistaken.

"Where was his body found?" I asked.

"Under Rivulet Bridge." They then laughed as they jokingly added, "It good for him, all them fellars should die like that."

"Like what? And what yuh mean by *them fellars*?"

The officer in charge then answered, "Well, we suspect that your friend Johnny was a pedophile because apparently he attacked a school boy and fell over the edge of the bridge. However, we assume the child wasn't hurt because we did not find the body, instead, we found your friend with a piece of the boy's school shirt clutched in his left hand and his pants leg torn."

I for one knew better, I knew the truth. And again it was my secret and mine alone to bear. The Jumbie Boy had appeared once again, this time to take the life and the legacy of a good, young man. To this day, I haven't had the courage to tell anyone. Perhaps now Johnny's story can be told as a warning or as good advice, take it as you wish. He has appeared to many and those who do not treasure their lives but give in to the fear of death will forever disappear as victims of the Jumbie Boy.

Accepted

I wish my reality was that my family was famous, living in a big house, no a mansion which would be four stories tall. My mansion would have ten bedrooms and six bathrooms with a game room, a movie room and, my personal favourite, a library. We would have fifty acres of land which would hold our swimming pool, tennis court, huge personal gardens and a dirt track to ride our dirt bikes on. I'd have all the latest in brand name clothing, shoes and high tech gadgets at my fingertips. Every weekend I'd hit the hottest clubs, liming with Chris Brown and Bow Wow, and be on the cover of *Sixteen Magazine* because everyone would want to be me. Or my reality could be just having a simple two-storey home with three rooms and two baths. There would be my mother, my father, my baby brother and me. My mom would be a teacher and my dad would be a manager of a huge business and my family would be well-off and my parents would love both my little brother and me very much. Oh how I wish my reality were any of these instead of–OWWW!

Nathifa Swan

I looked down on the ground at the can of Carib that hit me on the back of my head. I picked it up and looked at the culprit that threw it at me. My dad was standing in the door-way looking at me. When I observed him more closely, I discovered that he was drunk, again. The can of Carib should have been my first clue. His clothes are dishevelled and his eyes are all red and glassy which meant that he was out drinking all day again.

"Go and get me more Carib, chubby, I'm all out," slurred my dad.

He grabbed some money from his wrinkled-up shirt and threw it at me.

"Hurry up, you tub of lard, that's all you're good for any-ways."

And with that he staggered his way from my bedroom door to his recliner chair in the living room, like always.

My name is Isha Swan; I'm five-feet-nine, with dark brown hair and if you haven't guessed as yet, I'm mostly on the large side, and any reality would have been better than this one. My reality is living in a one bedroom apartment in Point Fortin, Trinidad and Tobago. I got the only bedroom because my dad just passes out on his recliner after he spends the whole day drinking, which is twenty-four hours a day, seven days a week, four weeks a month and twelve months per year.

I looked down on the ground at the money he threw at me. I sighed and picked it up. Why doesn't he throw some money my way to get some good school supplies or some decent clothes? Everyday is the same thing: "Go and get me some Carib, you fat pig," or something like, "Get me some more beer, fatty," always throwing the money at me and al-ways with some insult at the end.

I put the money in my pocket and stepped out of my room and put the lock on it, because if I don't my dad would come in and trash the place, like always. As I passed through the living room my dad had his recliner pushed back taking a nap, waiting for me to hurry my big behind, another one of his insults, to the bar out the road to buy him some more Carib. I sighed and walked out the front door, closing the door behind me. I slowly made my way to the bar thinking about how much my life sucks.

My mom died when I was six years old and my dad got depressed, when I say he got depressed, I mean he really got depressed. After they put her six feet under, he went on a rampage in our old home, which was a two bedroom apartment in San Fernando. He got rid of all her pictures, trashed the curtains off the windows, mom was really into arts and crafts and had all her creations all over the house. He went about the house just tearing them down and smashing them on the ground. When he was on his rampage of the house I ran to mom and dad's room and grabbed whatever I could of hers and transferred them to my room to get them out of dad's sight. When my dad was finished with his rampage, he collapsed in his room and cried all night long.

I heard his crying from my room, I let out all my own tears with him whilst staring at the only picture of my family that I was able to save from my dad's wrath. It was one with the three of us when I was five and we decided to go Gulf City for my birthday, it was one of the best days of my life. In the picture my mom was holding me whilst dad had some popcorn in his hair and he didn't know it, because I put some there when he wasn't looking. Mom and I were laughing at him and dad had this confused look on his face because he didn't know what we were laughing at, and of course that just made us laugh harder. I hugged the picture to my chest and took off my bedroom light to get ready for bed. I was going to miss my mom and I knew that my life was going to change without her around. I didn't know how right I was that night.

I was brought back to reality when I arrived at the bar. I went in and bought the six pack of Carib beer that my dad likes so much, said goodbye to the bartender and left. Even though I'm only fifteen years old and too young to be going in a bar to buy beer, the bartender knows my dad, since my dad is there every morning drinking the day away.

When I arrived back at the apartment, my dad was still passed out on his recliner snoring with some drool running down the side of his face, with him drooling I know that he has fallen into another of his drunken stupors and would be out for the rest of the night. I passed his chair to the corner which we call our "kitchen area" and put his six pack of Carib in the fridge to chill overnight.

I walked back into the living room and was about to enter my bedroom when something on the television caught my eye. The television was showing this fat person, like me, she had her own television show and she was interviewing some dude named T.I. who is supposedly some famous rapper or something. Due to my dad hogging the television everyday and school I'm not up to date on all that is current with music and stuff, I only know those celebrities that I hear people talk about in school. I watched as she laughed and how she had her audience captivated by her smile. I took a seat on the floor of the living room and watched the rest of her show. When her show was over I continued to sit on the ground and absorb what I just saw. I learned that her name was Mo'Nique and that she was proud of being big.

It was so refreshing to see someone with that size carry about themselves with such confidence and respect. She wasn't even afraid to show some skin, unlike me. I couldn't help but compare myself to her. She's outgoing while I am timid; she carries about herself with pride whilst I bow my head with shame. I couldn't help but wish that I was more like her. I looked at the time on the cable box and saw that it was 7 P.M.; I got up and made my way to my bedroom because I had to go to school tomorrow morning.

I was so glad that my dad was smart enough to rent out our house instead of selling it so that we would have some kind of income every month, because after mom died dad quit his job and picked up drinking, which takes up most of our money.

As I walked into the apartment with bags of groceries that I purchased after school with the money that dad gave me, I noticed that my dad wasn't home. I went to the kitchen area and put away the groceries and went to my room to change out of my school uniform. When I ventured out of my room again, my dad still was not home so I sat down on the ground and turned on the television.

I became addicted to Mo'Nique's talk show, my knowledge of celebrities has grown and I'm aware of a lot of fashion tips from her, from all the clothes that she wears that fit her figure just right. I watched as she talked with the cast of a comedy series called *The Game*. She was laughing and entertaining everyone.

Mo'Nique has become my idol and I want to be just like her. I go to the library to check out some self-help books to help motivate myself to learn how to accept who I am. Even though some of the exercises are weird and make me feel stupid, others are good and I do them on a daily basis. One of the exercises is for me to filter out all my thoughts and separate all the bad thoughts from all the good thoughts and minimise all my bad thoughts about myself and increase all my good thoughts. It was really surprising to me how much I put myself down on a daily basis, it was no wonder I felt so useless every day. Another exercise was for me to tell myself that I was a smart and beautiful person. I am a week into these exercises and I feel a lot better about myself.

I heard the lock on the front door turn and I scrambled to turn off the television and return to my room, I don't want my dad to see me watching television otherwise it would result in him screaming at me about how worthless I am and how I'm nothing but a sponge who soak up all his money, yeah right.

I reached my room just as my dad walked through the door; I was able to close my door before he noticed me. I looked towards my mom's sewing machine, which I was able to save from my dad's rampage, in the corner of my room. Since my dad doesn't give me money to buy clothes, I have to save up from the change I get when he gives me money to buy his beer and groceries, to buy cloth to make my own clothes.

I had always made my clothes loose so as not to show my lumps, but now watching Mo'Nique look fabulous in her outfits, I create my clothes to fit my shape perfectly so that it won't be too tight or too slack. I sat down at the sewing machine and got to work on putting the finishing touches on my first outfit to wear tomorrow for when I go to the library.

Saturday morning, when I got out of the shower, I looked at myself in the mirror, naked. I looked at myself for three seconds and turned away to put on my clothes. The self help books said that a way to help me accept myself was for me to look at myself naked in front of a full-length mirror and to tell myself that I am beautiful. But every time I look at myself all I hear is my father's voice telling me that I'm fat and disgusting and that all I'm good for is buying him beer and groceries; and to fight the tears that threaten to let loose I quickly turn away from my image and got dressed.

As I put on my outfit that I finished the night before, I couldn't help but notice the transformation that overcame my body. I have the shape of a two litre Coca Cola bottle, all I could do is look at myself and smile. I look hot and I feel wonderful. I put on my bag on my back and took one last look at myself before I walked out my bedroom door.

When I placed the lock on my bedroom door and turned around to leave I was shocked to see my dad standing behind me. He looked me over and an angry expression overcame his face. He reached out his hand and grabbed the front of my blouse and pulled me close to him.

"I knew I was missing some of *my* money; what the hell were you thinking stealing money from me to buy your fat ass new clothes?" Dad paused in his rant to look me over once more before saying, "I'm surprise you even found any that could fit your big behind. What size is that XXXXXXXL?"

I was hurt by his harsh words. Why can't I get back my old dad, the one who used to tuck me in at night and tell me that he loved me? As my dad continued to insult me, tears gather at the edge of my eyes but I refused to let them fall, I keep repeating to myself that I was smart and beautiful and that helped to keep my tears at bay.

"You are nothing but a worthless piece of—"

Something finally snapped in me, I am fed up of feeling useless, I'm fed up of my own father putting me down every chance he gets and I am sick and tired putting myself down. I broke out of my dad's hold, head down, with my hands balled into fists and said:

"I am NOT worthless, I am a smart and beautiful individual and I have value; you're just too blind to see that."

I looked at my dad's face and when I saw his surprised expression it gave me the courage to continue:

"Do you have any idea how much it hurts to have your dad say hurtful things to you all the time? How he cares more about drinking than how his daughter is doing in school and how he cares more about buying Carib beer than getting her school supplies or clothes. I have to say thank goodness for free secondary education otherwise I wouldn't be able to go to school."

I looked my dad in the eyes, something I haven't done in a long time, and saw sadness in them. I was surprised to see that emotion there and I realised something.

"You miss mom, don't you dad?" I asked.

I thought my dad was going to deny it and walk away; instead he looked at me with a heartbroken look and went to the fridge to grab a Carib. I knew now why my dad drank all the time, to forget about everything that happened with mom, and that got me angry. When my dad returned in the living room, I stalked up to him, grabbed his can of Carib and threw it across the room.

"You can't accept that mom is gone so you bury your misery with alcohol? Do you have any idea how stupid that is? Mom was killed coming home from work because of a drunk driver! He just came out of some party drunk off his ass and barrelled right into her, and you think drinking is the best solution?"

I looked at my dad and saw the tears forming at his eyes. I walked over to him and put my hand on his chest and said:

"You need to accept that mom is gone dad, you also need to accept that drinking isn't the way to drown out all your problems."

I looked deep into dad's eyes and continued my little speech:

"I love you dad, and so does mom."

Dad looked at me so sharply that I thought his head would snap.

"Just because mom is gone doesn't mean that she does not love us dad. You know and I know that mom would not want you living in misery over her so you just have to accept that mom is gone and move on; but always carry her in your heart because even though mom's gone she is not forgotten."

After my little speech I gave a small smile for my dad and that just opened the flood gate on his emotions. My dad hugged me and broke down. He cried out years of depression on me, saying that he was sorry over and over, and I just held him knowing that everything was going to be okay from now on.

One year later I was standing in front of the full-length mirror in my room, looking at myself naked. Before I couldn't stand to look at myself but now I can't stop looking at my beautiful refection. I smiled and put on my clothes. My dad still drinks but not as much as he used to, but he's working on lowering the drinking some more; I'm proud of him for trying. We still live in the one bedroom apartment; dad wasn't ready to move back into our home in San Fernando, I have to admit, neither am I. I was content having my dad back, no more insults, and for finally having some confidence in myself. I am thankful for a lot of things but I am mostly thankful for finally being accepted.

Crazy Mary

The great fiery eye slowly opens and looks down on the village of Morne Alto, seeking to give direction to all of its inhabitants. One of the first persons to awake and use the assistance it provides is a woman who from all appearances looks normal. Dressed in a formal dress with shoes and bags to match, head held high, walking as one who understands the meaning of the word etiquette. She is walking the road in the dim light; going to… she stops, begins talking to herself rapidly in a whisper, then throws her head back and laughs out loud in the quiet of the morning.

"Crazy Mary again!" the awakened inhabitants of the houses on the street will say, some will say more, words that I cannot write here.

"They should lock her away, that woman real mad yes," others will say, but Mary troubles no one.

Crazy Mary is an intrinsic part of the village, I have known her all of my life and her laugh is etched in my mind like the words of a popular song. She is not like the homeless people

I see walking the pavements of my island's cities, she is different. Mary lives at the end of Prosper Avenue, in one of the largest houses in the village, which sits on the most acreage owned by any private citizen for miles around. Both house and land are overgrown with weeds and are in a sad state of disrepair, however even in this condition some of its past grandeur shines through. Marble columns, hand sculptured fountains, hedges and ceiling-high windows have avoided the descent into the mental state of its owner.

Crazy Mary is always dressed as I described, her clothes are all handmade and are of quality fabric which due to the ravages of time and lack of proper care have faded, the sewing giving way in many places. But Mary looks dignified in them as she walks the streets, striding, looking straight ahead. There is one thing Mary does with which no one can find fault, though it brings traffic to a halt every time she does it, she will dance in the street. Mary will suddenly and unexpectedly stop, draw herself into a dancing pose and begin to execute the most fluid and precise ballroom dance steps I have ever seen, Foxtrot, Rumba, Waltz, Polka, one-step, Salsa, and more. Some people will be imitating the steps, others watch fascinated, and those who know the dances will clap out music. Crazy Mary is harmless. The village dance instructor will walk away from this dancing display saying:

"Is better I go mad and then teach people dancing, Crazy Mary does put me to shame!"

I have always had more contact with Crazy Mary than most people in the village, my family's land bounds Mary's so I see her when she is at home and outside, plus she comes to our gate three times a day to receive food. My mom also gives her bath and washing soap. She will come to our gate and stand there the picture of decorum and wait until we give her the food, my mom will sometimes give the food, bath and washing soap to my sister or me to give to her. Mary will accept it, smile and head back to her house.

I have always been curious about the story which surrounds Crazy Mary and the reason my mother makes it her duty to give her food, bath and washing soap, purchasing extra at the supermarket for this. I kept looking for the opportunity to ask her the reason for her actions when circumstances intervened causing her to tell me without my having to ask.

One lunch time Mom finishes her cooking, places Mary's food into a container and keeps looking for her to come out of her house and begin walking down the street; it was my day to give her the food. She sees Mary come out and begin walking down to us.

"Brian, she is coming down, go to the gate with the food and wait for her there, please."

I stop helping my sister lay the table, take the food, walk down the steps and begin walking toward the gate. As I get closer to the gate I see that the neighbour opposite us has a light blue 1960 Chevrolet convertible with matching color interior parked in front his house. I stand there admiring it when I reach the gate, then call out to my mom and sister:

"Mom, Rita come and see what Mr Thomas has parked in front of his house this time."

My mom and sister soon walk into the front porch; mom takes one look at the car and yells:

"Oh God no, no!" with a look of horror on her face, then looks in the direction Crazy Mary is coming from.

"Brian, carry the food to her NOW! Go now Brian!"

I try to rush through the gateway with the food but my slippers caught in the wire at the bottom of the gate and I stumble, fall and spill the food.

"Oh God no, no not now!" my mother cries as I lay face down in the road.

I get to my knees and Crazy Mary is standing looking down at me, she then looks up at my mother, studies her face for a minute and then slowly turns around and sees the car. Her mouths opens wide, no sound comes out at first, then the most horrible scream I have ever heard in my entire life comes out. She sways almost falling and then runs off screaming toward her house. I remain kneeling, trembling, too scared to move as I watch Crazy Mary running. One by one the neighbours come out and watch Mary running toward her house, she runs inside, slams the door shut and continues to scream from inside.

My mom and sister run down the steps into the road and help me to get to my feet. Mom is examining my cut knees and elbows, but she is breathing heavy and sweating, she is very angry, I know the signs well, I stay silent. She turns to Mr Thomas who is now standing behind her enquiring about the recent events.

"Erica, what—"

He is cut short: "Do you know what your stupid show-off ways have done to that poor woman?"

"I... I... I... I—"

"The man who tricked her, shattered her heart, stole her money and caused her to lose her mind drove a car exactly like that one, that car may even be the same one!"

"I... I... I... I—"

"Yes Mr Show-off, say something, say something!"

Mr Thomas stops trying to say anything, turns, gets into the car, starts it and reverses down the street into the main road and drives away. My mom is crying as she looks at Mary's house and listens to her ongoing screams, she does not go into our house until the screaming subsides. As she sits on the steps waiting, she tells Mary's story:

"I grew up on this street but lived closer to the main road. Mary Mac Milan always lived in that house, she was born there. As far back as I remember her family owned that land and were rich, it was a large estate producing all types of crops and providing employment for most of the villagers, they had business in the city also. Mary was always the best dressed female for miles around and went to the best schools; she learned cooking, etiquette, fashion and ballroom dancing there. As a young girl I remember her being elegantly dressed and having chauffeur-driven convertible cars, she would pass and wave at us as we were playing or walking to places. She would bake cookies and muffins, and give them to the children in the village from time to time, but we on the street got the most. Her house was like a castle, not as it is now; it was busy all year, with people coming and going often. The best time of the year for the house and the village was the annual harvest fair and ball, this road would be buzzing with activity, workers building this, cooking that, musicians rehearsing and the dancers practicing for the ballroom dancing contest. This contest was the highlight of the season; contestants came from all parts of the island to compete against one person, yes, Ms Mary Mac Milan with her partner. Mary was impossible to beat up until she lost her mind, that ANIMAL did it to her. We would put aside everything when the contest was on,

35

just to see Mary dance and bring those outsiders to tears after seeing her style.

One day this light blue convertible drove up the street with the best looking and debonair man we had ever seen. It appeared to be love at first sight; he drove in one evening a few weeks before the annual harvest fair and ball, and did not leave until he had tricked her. She was then living alone, both her parents had died, so he began living in the house, they would go for morning and evening drives cuddled up close in the backseat. She was so happy then, especially when he asked her to become his wife, they were to be married immediately after the fair. She gave him money to do some business in the city while she remained here to do the wedding preparations, I saw him drive by that morning, and he waved to me. As the wedding day grew closer and he did not return Mary began to worry, so did the entire village, a few days before the wedding day, she left to find him fearing he may have been hurt in some way. We were in the house still preparing for the wedding when she returned, chased everyone out, and then proceeded to destroy everything related to the wedding. She threw out the food, burnt all the decorations, then stripped apart her unfinished wedding dress; we cried as we watched her do it. We later learnt he was married and had come here just to steal her money.

Mary was never the same after that, she gradually let the estate go to ruins, fired workers every day, closed the city businesses and stayed inside the house most of the time. The harvest day came and passed without anything being done, it was on that day one year later she began screaming and started walking the road the next day. From that day to now I have been giving her food every day; I care for her because she was kind to me. When this parcel of land became available for sale, your father bought it; he felt it would be better for Mary and me if I was living closer to her. We were living on Canaan Road; she had to cross the main road to get to my house. Your father believed it was not safe for her to be crossing that road three times a day. You were born here."

"Is this land the reason daddy took the job up the islands?"

"Yes, work paying enough to pay off for the land and house became hard to find in the village so we decided it was best for him to go to Union where his skills were in greater demand."

"You both did this for Mary?"

"She needed someone to look out for her; I am the only 'family' she has. We tried to locate her relatives when she got sick but the lawyers could not find any. Her parents came from abroad and the lawyers could not find out where that was plus she was an only child. The lawyers asked her whom she trusted, she called my name and that was that."

My mom listens, the screams have stopped.

"Let us get some sleep now; I will see her tomorrow morning when she comes for her breakfast."

The familiar figure of Crazy Mary does not stride down the road the following morning, her breakfast remains on the kitchen counter. My mom is sad and silent for the entire morning; she however packs a lunch for Mary.

"Rita, Brian, come with me to give Mary her lunch."

The three of us walk to the house in silence; I try even more to picture in my mind the splendour of the house and land before Mary's illness. I am now able to connect the seemingly out of place objects covered with weeds in the yard; I can see tables, large pots and other utensils, nothing was ever removed from the yard. As we walk up the driveway, my eyes see things I never noticed before; the house has come alive to me. We walk to the double front doors; my mom knocks hard and shouts:

"Mary! Mary! It's me! Erica! I have your lunch!"

An eternity seems to pass before Mary opens the door, in shock we look at the woman standing before us, uncombed hair, in a battered robe with a very sad looking, unwashed face; we gasp. Never have I seen Mary in this condition and judging from my mom's and sister's reaction, neither have they.

"Here Mary, take your lunch. I put in some muffins. Do you have soap to bathe and wash?"

Slowly Mary head moves, nodding yes.

"Okay, eat, bathe, put on a beautiful dress and I will bring you dinner."

Mary turns and walks with dragging steps back into the house, we stand looking at her fade into the dim interior of the house. We then turn and walk slowly home, my mom is crying silently, my sister and I hug her as we make that painful return journey. Our afternoon is a repeat of the morning, no humming and singing from my mother, the jolly woman I have known my entire life, except when you rub her the wrong way, is absent. Six o'clock arrives and it is time to deliver Mary's dinner. I am helping my mom place the lunch into a bag when my sister runs into the kitchen totally excited.

"Mommy, mommy, Cr… Mary is standing at the gate, mommy she is…" and shakes her head from side to side. My mom and I rush past her, reach the front porch and stand there in complete silence as we look at Mary.

Mary Mac Milan is dressed in a beautiful, pink, flowing evening gown, with elbow-length gloves and a large handbag to match; around her neck is a pearl necklace with matching bracelets. On her head is a broad evening hat, a bit worn but still exquisite, her hair, streaked with grey, cascades from under it to her shoulder blades; on her shoulder, spinning slowly, is a pink and white parasol. Mary is standing there head held high, back erect, looking up at us with a smile on her face. Tears are running down our cheeks as we continue to enjoy the portrait before us. I turn, go into the kitchen get the bag with Mary's lunch and go to the gate to join my mom and sister. All of the neighbours seem to be out in the street now, looking at Mary and whispering softly. I drape the handle bag over her arm, she nods, turns around, looks at the spot where the car was parked yesterday, then looks up at Mr Thomas, nods, turns, faces her house and walks away as only Mary can.

All of us living on Prosper Avenue watch Crazy Mary, no, Mary Mac Milan take an evening stroll to her house, walk up the driveway, gracefully open the door, look back at us, curtsey and enter, closing the door slowly behind her.

The muddy shoes

The apartment stopped radiating the comfort it once held when he moved in three years ago. It was on the upper floor of a building in a seaside town. A four burner gas stove he hardly used stood in a corner with grease-stained walls. A soot-coated pot and several long spoons hung from a wall-mounted rack. A white single-door refrigerator he knew too well was dotted with fruit-shaped magnets, and the simple chair and table told of a lone occupant. An adjourning room contained a small metal frame bed he made up only when his mother visited. Both rooms held his worldly possessions, and they exuded all signs of masculine habitation.

Business in the area had picked up, and the honking cars, the non-stop chatter of tourists, and loud music from the si-dewalk cafes that sprung up overnight, all drowned the sounds of the waves that lulled him to sleep.

Lately, his nights were pierced with a strange dream. He was chased on the beach by hovering forms of human faces, and they pursued him onto the rocks until he fell into the crashing waves. He always woke up reaching for the scar on his arm.

He worked as a line supervisor at Ryan and Sons, the town's fish packing plant. It took him just three years to move up, and at twenty one he was the youngest supervisor.

"Andrew you left the air conditioning unit running all day." The landlord ascended the narrow stairs.

"I'll remember next time." He avoided prolong conversations.

"Well it's costing me money…" The baldhead disappeared back down the creaking steps.

His mother never liked the apartment and even less the landlord. She wanted him to come back home and pleaded at each visit. He refused each time. The last time she came the pleading escalated into an argument, and she left in tears. He wanted to call and apologise, but he never liked calling home. The home-cooked meal she brought, as she did at every visit, was still in the refrigerator. He felt guilty to eat it.

His cell phone rang.

"Andrew, can you pick Jason up from school? Anil is working late and we may not get there on time."

"Sure sis."

A quick change out of his work clothes, and he headed for the school. It took ten minutes, on most evenings, for the walk down the street lined with souvenir shops, through the town's park, and into the school's compound.

The evening wind from the ocean grew sturdy and tugged at his clothes. The same ocean wind blew through his window and kept him cool. Most of the shops along the street were closed and a few last minute shoppers lingered at the opened ones. A sprinkle of rain fell but was chased away by the increasing wind. The clouds were forming a grey cover overhead, and he knew a heavy downpour would soon follow.

He was drenched when he reached the park. Sprinkle turned to heavy rain, heavier by the second, and drops penetrated the ground with drumming splatter. The tall thicket of trees swayed in the blustering wind and scattered leaves across the park. The ground was soft and muddy and slowed his pace. There was a bright flash of light and an overhead rumble grew louder and nearer. He was caught in a thunderstorm. He took shelter in the park's gazebo. It was an open wooden structure with a leaking metal roof, and offered little protection. He looked for the school through the rain, but could not tell the direction and felt like a lost sailor looking for land. The rain and wet clothes clung to his cold skin, and he crouched down on the wet planked floor. He stared at the trail of mud and then shifted his gaze to his shoes. They were muddy. He froze, and, as if by instinct, felt an eerie shiver run through his entire body.

Four years earlier, he had finished high school and he routinely tended his mother's kitchen garden. He watered the plants with rainwater collected in a barrel which was kept full by a makeshift galvanised spout. She was an avid planter, and planted anything she could use in the kitchen. The string beans, the tomatoes, the peppers, and the melange all ended in the family's pot. She was contented her son was not afraid to get his hands dirty.

On evenings, he and his mother sat in the back porch of their small-frame wooden house and looked at the day's work done in the garden. A couple of small houses stood beyond the garden and cast long shadows across its beds and up to the steps. She wore her old woollen sweater and drank tea from her favourite rose-patterned teacup and spoke of the next day's chores. He never finished his, and the half-filled cup got cold with the last rays of the sun. His father only joined them after dark, and he left his parents sitting there before he went to bed.

He spent the weekends at the Regal Mall with his friends. It was five miles from the village, and his father drove him there and picked him up after a few hours.

Weekend came and he and his father headed to the Regal Mall. The rain was falling and he remembered it was in that kind of weather that his father had driven to the hospital. They had all gone to see Jason, the newest addition to the family.

The wet road made the driving difficult, and the car wobbled slightly at times. The drive was slow and his father decided to take a shortcut. Gibson Road passed through a small wooded area and was narrow and had potholes that became small pools of dirty water. It was usually used to avoid traffic on the main road. About halfway along they neared a sharp corner and suddenly an oncoming car, trying to avoid a pothole, sped towards them. His father instantly hit the brake pedal and swerved to avoid a collision.

It was too late. He saw everything in slow motion. The car skidded off the road, turned over several times, and landed in a deep ditch. The deafening thud of metal against earth, the sound of shattering glass, and the quickness of it all stunned him. His father was slumped on the steering wheel, motionless. He felt a sharp pain in his left arm, his eyes closed and everything jumped to black.

When he regained consciousness it was night. The pain in his left arm was intense. Water from the swollen ditch was rushing and filling inside the car. He crawled out. His father's door was stuck, and he tried with all the strength in both arms. After the third struggle it opened with a sharp swing, and he pulled him through the rushing water and onto the embankment.

Blood covered his father's face and the rain trickled it down into a red pool. He raised his head and made a gurgling sound and spat a mouthful of blood. He tried to say something but coughed up more blood.

"Andrew… are you alright? There's blood on your arm…" Blood oozed from a gash on his forehead and onto the mud.

"I'm okay dad. Just don't move too much…" He shifted his father to lie straight. He never faced a serious emergency before, and was confused as what to do next.

"You'll have to get help son." His father pointed to the road above as a pair of headlights appeared and disappeared.

He ran up the muddy slope, its grass flattened by the crushed car, slipping twice before he came on the roadway. It was empty. The glow of the moon behind the clouds cast a dim light on the wet ground. Tall trees lined the road, and their shadows moved with the wind. The main road was a quarter mile away, and he ran towards it. He felt the stony ground grew harder under his feet with every stride and was out of breath when he saw the lights of an approaching car.

"Stop! Stop! Please stop!" He ran alongside the car.

The car did not slow down. He knelt down at the side of the road, cold and helpless. A soft whirring sound soon became louder. The car was reversing.

"Good Lord! Are you lost young man?" The bewildered driver quickly rolled down the window.

"We got into an accident and my father..." He held on tightly to the door.

The man helped him put his father to lie on the backseat. His father stared at him without blinking and muttered something under his breath. His head rested on Andrew's lap.

As they drove he notice someone was seated next to the man. The head of black hair turned, and he saw a young girl looking at him. She took a long look at his injured father. She did not flinch at the sight of blood.

At the hospital the doctor rushed his father into the operating theatre. A nurse attended to his arm. He had forgotten about the pain. It took six stitches to close the cut in his arm. The man and the young girl waited with him.

"My dad has a cell phone. You should call your mother." The young girl pointed to the man.

His mother was hysterical.

He waited for the doctor to bring word of his father, something, anything. He could not sit. He could not stand and stay still. He paced the corridor hoping to catch a glimpse of the doctor. When he could not bear it any longer he found a corner and sat down on the cold tiled floor. He pulled his knees close to his face. He saw his shoes. They were caked with mud and dried blood.

The girl came in front of him. She was younger than him, about fourteen, and had skinny arms. Her yellow dress was dotted with honeybees on large sunflowers and her hair was neatly combed and tucked behind her ears. She had a plain face and her dark eyes seemed to look right through him. She

45

reminded him of rich preppy kids that attended boarding school.

"You must be hungry. My dad can get you a sandwich from the cafeteria."

"I'm not hungry." His downcast eyes focused back on the tiled floor.

"My father never takes the shortcut, but the traffic was too much. Luckily we saw you." She moved closer.

"You saved us. Thank you. I thought he was never going to stop."

"He was afraid at first."

"I understand. A stranger asking for help on a lonely road at night will test anyone's goodwill."

"My father is a kind soul." She looked towards her father at the nurse's desk.

"If you were driving would you have stopped?" He knew she was too young to drive.

"I would have. And if I see you in distress again, I will save you." She sounded sympathetic yet confident.

He wanted to ask her name, where she lived, but her father kept looking in their direction.

The funeral was four days later. His father never recovered. Lost too much blood the doctor said. His mother cried for the four days. All the people from the village attended the funeral. He thought the flames from the pyre would burn the memory of the accident from his mind, but it never did.

He hardly spoke to anyone for days and the guilt of asking his father to take him to the mall played like a non-stop record in his head. There stood no tombstone to cry at and ask forgiveness and he wished he could go back in time and change everything.

His mother coped with her grief in her own way. She had no long conversations with him or his sister, and she was obsessed with keeping the house clean. She kept more and more to herself and carried a sullen look on her face.

The kitchen garden was unattended and overgrown with short, thick grass. The tomatoes dried up, the melange grew stunted, and the peppers dropped off the plants.

The back porch was empty on evenings.

A garlanded picture of his father hung on the living room wall, and he avoided looking at it. He never stayed long inside the house. He feared the picture would come to life and speak, and blame him. Sadness grew thick in the house, and it choked him.

Everyone told him he was now the man of the house. It was too much for him to bear, and he wanted to get as far away as he could from the village.

The thunder cracked like a whip, and more rain dashed inside the gazebo. He looked up and saw the floating faces from his dreams. It was his father's with those large eyes staring and not blinking. It then turned into his mother's and came closer and grew larger. It suddenly turned into the face of the young girl in the yellow dress and covered him in a flash. It confused him, and he jumped up and bolted out of the gazebo. Instantly there was a bright flash that blinded him and a loud crashing sound. He froze in his tracks. He slowly looked back and what he saw frightened him. The gazebo was blown apart, and flaming pieces were strewn on the ground. Smoke and hissing steam rose from what little was left of the standing structure.

He quickly got back the use of his legs and ran through the rain towards the school like a man possessed. He ran deliberately through every puddle of water he could find on the street. His shoes were clean when he reached the gate.

The school was a grey three-storey concrete building next to the town's police station. His sister wanted a safe neighbourhood for Jason. The lobby where the kids waited for their parents was on the first floor, and he was winded at the top of the stairs. Mrs. Davis, the principal's secretary, would be with the kids, she always was. He entered the room and startled its four occupants.

"Look! It's Uncle Andrew!" The youngest let go of his mother's hand and ran to meet him.

The oldest had a long look at his extremely wet attire. "Son, you'll catch your death in this weather."

I almost did, two more seconds in the gazebo, and I would not be standing in front of you mom, he said to himself. He decided not to tell them of his close encounter.

She took off his wet jacket and pulled out a handkerchief from her black leather handbag and proceeded to wipe his wet hair as if he was still a child. "I was wrong in asking you to come home."

"I'm sorry about the arguing."

"I lost your father and I didn't want to lose you too." She wiped his face.

"You will not lose me, mom."

"I have been thinking it's time to let you go. And this is the time." She smiled, the first time since the funeral. She combed his hair with her fingers and said no more.

He was sad and happy and relieved all in one. It meant no more arguments with her, but it also meant he was his own responsibility.

Mrs. Davis was behind the desk near the principal's office. The door was open. He never saw it open in all the times he came. He peered inside. Stacks of paper and a reading lamp were on a desk and behind it an empty leather armchair. A large gold-framed picture hung on the wall.

"I know that person."

Mrs. Davis shifted from her desk and took a quick glance. "Andrew, everyone knows the principal." She sat back down and signalled his sister to sign the permission book.

"No. I meant the girl in the yellow dress. She must be what, eighteen by now?"

"Eighteen? Who? Oh, she would have been thirty four this year."

"Thirty... what did you say?"

"Thirty four years. Poor girl, she died twenty years ago in a car accident on Gibson Road."

Lovingly mischievous

"I need your help." That was one thing that Daniel, the God of Love, never thought he'd hear his mischievous, blond friend say.

"Excuse me?" Dani asked, his blue-streaked brown hair shimmering in the small amount of sunlight that got through the window of his rooftop pad on Earth.

"Oh you just want me to say it again, don't you? I'm not an idiot you know," Raymond responded as his companion grunted in response. "Okay fine, I, your mischievous best friend, need your everlasting love bringing majestic self's help. Is that enough filling for your ego yet?"

Daniel smirked, "Whatever, what do you want my help for anyway?"

"It's a mortal, a mortal girl to be exact."

"Are you trying to get her to fall for you? Please say no."

"Eww, a mortal? That's disgusting! I'd rather fall for you."

"No thank you."

"Wiseass, don't make me call you Cupid."

Daniel's eyes darkened, promising certain death. "You wouldn't dare."

"You know for the God of Love, you can be pretty scary sometimes."

"You have obviously never been in love. Anyway what about this mortal girl and why do you need my help?" The brunette stood up, a smirk plastered on his face as he approached his robed friend. He leant in close and whispered in his ear, "Tell me that you can at least handle a mere mortal... Loki, or should I call you Hermes?"

Ray pushed his friend back slightly. "Ugh, you know I hate that name! This mortal is special. Xander is making me waste my mischief on good deeds, to teach mortals lessons as he put it. What a stupid idea, I mean who died and made him our leader?"

"Zeus," Dani answered.

"That was rhetorical."

"I know."

Ray stuck out his tongue at his friend.

Daniel rolled his eyes in response, "How childish, what are you not telling me?"

"What do you mean?"

"You seem to forget that unlike you, I am not stupid. I know that Xander never gets involved in the day-to-day business of gods, unless they do something to get on his bad side."

"Well," the blond chuckled, scratching his head nervously, "I may have set loose magically bewitched mud, spewing wild pigs in the God of Music's sky palace and they may have gotten mud all over the library's scrolls."

"What? How could you accidentally do tha– you know what I don't even want to know, continue with your story. I'm getting bored."

"Fine, fine, as part of my punishment, Xander sometimes picks the mortals he wants me to work with. This mortal is one of the ones he picked. Her name is Ashley. She needs to learn how to be herself. She hides herself and her true potential so others will accept her. She is supposed to be destined for great things but if she continues the way she is she'll never achieve it."

"Okay, I still don't know what this has to do with me."

"Isn't love supposed to be selfless?" Ray gave his companion an accusing look.

"It is, I'm not." The brunette tapped his fingers loudly on his armrest showing his impatience.

"I want you to help me bewitch her."

"No."

"Come on."

"No."

"Listen I already talked to Xander, he thinks that your common sense will rub off on me and make sure that I don't go overboard. Come on man, help me out here."

"No."

"Okay fine, I'll make a deal with you. If you help me out, I won't play any pranks on you for a month."

"For a year."

"What? An entire year?! Okay fine."

"Alright I'll help you, now take me to the girl."

Ashley stood timidly behind her friends, her arms filled with books that belonged to her so-called friends. Her black hair in a tight bun, her uniform neat and her skirt ended at the required length for the girls in her school. Her dark skin was flawless as was her smile but she wouldn't say any of those things about herself.

Raymond and Daniel, disguised as substitute teachers, stood looking on.

"Tell me again why we have to act as teachers now?"

"Because some dumbass decided to set wild pigs in Xander's house also, so he bound us to Earth and took away our cloaking abilities until the task is complete."

"So unfair!"

"I know, having an idiot like you teach these kids, there goes their future."

"Fuc–" Ray started but stopped as Ashley and her friends started speaking.

"So Ashley," began a redheaded girl who was leaning against the locker in front of her, "did you do the chemistry homework for today?"

"Umm, Kathy, yes I did, but–"

"Okay thanks!" The girl grabbed Ashley's bag and searched through it. She pulled out a notebook and began copying down answers. "You should change some of these; I don't want us to have the same answers."

"Okay, but–"

"Hey Ashley, don't forget that you promised to hand in those petitions for me." Another girl had come up to her.

"What? I don't remem–"

"Ashley come on, you don't want to disappoint everyone do you?"

"No, but–"

"Then it's settled." The girl pushed a stack of papers into Ashley's already-filled hands.

"Pathetic," Daniel muttered.

"I know," Ray shook his head agreeing; he too had seen enough, "Let's bewitch her now."

Daniel nodded and started whispering a spell, "From now until love is found–"

Ray continued, "Your timid speech shall now be bound–"

"Until you learn to be yourself–"

"You will randomly say what no one else–"

"Would ever dare to do or say–"

"But yet you'll say it anyway–"

"Only love of self will break this curse–"

"One, two, three, now do your worst!" Ray ended.

They put the tips of their fingers together and Ashley sneezed three times.

"Hey are you okay?" The redhead known as Kathy asked, adding before she could get a response, "It doesn't matter; I'll be needing your Biology homework too."

"No."

"Ashley you don't want to… what did you just say?"

"Do your own homework." Ashley grabbed the paper with the copied homework and tore it to shreds, dropping the petitions and everything else that was in her hand in the process. "And you deliver the damn petitions yourself. That is, unless you want me to destroy them too."

"What the hell is wrong with you?" The girl asked, shocked.

"Huh?" Ashley snapped out of it. "I don't know, Janet. I didn't mean too… at least I didn't… I'm sorry I–"

"Well," Janet started to think it over, "don't let it happen again."

"Okay, once I don't have to see your ugly face again," she said before she could stop herself.

"This is getting good!" The mischievous god could barely contain himself as he tapped his friend heartily on his back and chuckled.

"Whatever," the love god replied before walking off, shaking his head.

Ashley didn't understand. She used to be so good at hiding how she really felt, when those girls mistreated her. Now it was a mix of her actually saying what she thought, in a way; that she never dared.

"That's so cool! You're finally sticking up for yourself. I'm so proud of you," her best friend, Joslen, said while nudging her shoulder playfully. They were sitting in the cafeteria and as usual Joslen was talking while eating. She wore three bracelets on each hand and her hair was purple and black. Her uniform shirt was always tucked half in and half out and she sported a nose ring. They were complete opposites in the way they dressed and spoke, but they had been friends since they had met four years ago. Sometimes Ashley would find herself wishing that she could be as cool as Joslen and not care what people thought about her.

"Noo, it's not cool. I was mean to Kathy and Janet. Who knows if they'll ever talk to me again. What if they try to get back at me?"

"Ah, who cares! What's the worst that could happen?"

"I don't want to know."

The first week was the worst. Kathy came up to our cursed friend, trying to get her homework again. She called behind her a few times but the brunette kept walking. She didn't want a repeat of what had happened before.

Finally she managed to corner Ashley, "Hey didn't you hear me calling you?"

No answer.

"Oookay well, I need your Math homework."

"No." Ashley looked towards the floor. She was trying to fight whatever it was inside her that was making her speak out like that.

"What? Listen, Ashley, I don't know what your problem is these days and frankly I don't care, but you are really pushing your luck." She smiled, adding sweetly, "You don't want to end up on my bad side, trust me."

By now the hallways were full of students chatting with their peers and getting ready for their classes to start. Most of them paused and stared in surprise as Ashley began laughing loudly and excessively. Kathy looked at her like she was going crazy.

"You... ha ha ha ha... your bad side... ha ha ha ha ha... now that's funny." Ashley waved her hands around pretending to be scared. "Wow, I haven't laughed that hard since... well, actually, I've never laughed that much at all. Thanks, Kath, I didn't know that you wanted to be a comedian." She brushed past her and headed towards her locker when a hand on her shoulder stopped her and spun her around.

"Listen you–"

"No, you listen" – Ashley's eyes darkened slightly as she cut Kathy off – "I may have put up with your crap before but now is different. Now, if you ever dare touch me, like you did just now, I will introduce you to my bad side. Right now this is my bad side on a good day, you don't ever want to see it on a bad day, trust me. You, my friend, you're a bully, and although it's not my fault that you're dumb and a loser I would still be willing to put aside the past and tutor you in the subjects that you need help with. However, if you ever ask me for my homework again, I *will* break your face."

She turned and walked off, a genuine smile plastered on her face. Somewhere during her speech the curse seemed to ease up and she started speaking her mind.

She ignored Kathy's voice coming from behind her, calling her a freak from a distance and continued walking on and smiling.

"I think we've created a monster," Ray said to Daniel who was standing next to the water fountain.

"Humph, speak for yourself," Daniel answered before he chuckled slightly to himself.

The second week was a little better. By now Ashley had gotten used to the popular kids and some of Kathy's other friends calling her a freak. She had also started to get used to the two new substitute teachers, who always seemed to be around watching her. It was probably only her imagination anyway.

She told Joslen about it, but she just ruled it off as one of Ashley's wannabe fantasies.

"You mean you wish two of the hottest teachers in the school were stalking you. Come on admit it; it's okay. Besides, we have all had that dream."

Ashley giggled thinking about how the female student body acted towards the new teachers and she knew that Joslen was probably right about them all wanting to be with them. She got up and left the lunchroom, heading over to her locker.

"That's funny." She didn't know why she never said anything weird around Joslen. Maybe that was because she was always herself around her.

She tried to avoid anyone who might make her lose control but she didn't have to do much of that since most people kept out of her way anyway. Only now and then she found herself saying something out loud that she'd usually only say in her head to herself.

The curse was even affecting how she acted with the teachers and even herself. The teachers complimented her on her efforts to participate more in class. She was stunned when she realised that somehow she'd gotten up and signed herself up for both tennis and cheerleading. Everyone was shocked that she turned out for tryouts, even herself. Her routine was more than good enough to more than impress them. No one besides Joslen knew that she used to be a gymnast. She even made it on the tennis team. It was strange but after she became more outspoken and started to do the things that she had always wanted to, but was too afraid to try, people started to notice her for good reasons and not for being a pushover and a freak.

By the end of the second week, some people even began to talk to her. She was making friends and she was very happy about it. Better yet, the more her outbursts forced her to be herself, the more she learned how valuable she was.

Soon the outbursts were happening less frequently. It didn't stop her from voicing her thoughts whenever she thought she needed too though.

It had been three weeks since the curse had been placed and people started to treat Ashley differently. She started to realise who her true friends were, and, somehow, in the middle of the craziness, she started to realise her true potential. Somewhere inside it clicked that whatever was happening to her wasn't a bad thing, it was actually helping her. So slowly but surely she started to find herself and the spell started wearing off a little each day.

"Hey look!" Ray ran up to Daniel, ignoring the stares the few remaining students who had yet to leave were giving him. He grabbed his shirt and practically dragged him into an empty classroom. He held out his hands for Daniel to see. "I can go invisible again. I guess since the spell is wearing off we are getting back our full powers."

"Looks to me like Xander is feeling generous," Daniel summed up.

"Well this certainly worked out much faster than I thought it would."

"Yeah me too, she even found herself some real friends."

"I'm confused though, how come she didn't find true love?"

"She did, she needed to find true love for *herself* to break the curse, not a boyfriend. Anyway at the rate she's going, by the end of the month I think she will be cured completely and I can get rid of you."

The brunette sighed.

"Aww. Now Daniel, you know you'd miss me."

"Yeah? Keep telling yourself that. I am going home and you're not invited."

"You're just saying that." Ray dismissed the statement, knowing that even if Daniel said that he wasn't invited now, if he were to tag along anyway, he wouldn't be stopped. They had been friends long enough for him to know Daniel better than most people. "Which home? You have like five different houses, man."

"Stop exaggerating, I only have two, one on earth and my sky palace."

"It doesn't matter, besides, why do you have a house on earth for anyway?"

"Well idiot, sometimes being the God of Love means blending in with mortals and getting to know how they think and behave."

"Sounds boring..."

"Of course you'd think so. You don't do anything."

"Hey being mischievous all the time is hard, you know!"

"Chi, yeah sure it is, anyway I'm going back to my sky palace."

"Oh... ha... about that. Well, you see... the pigs may have gotten into your palace too."

"Ray," Daniel practically growled, "you'd better be joking."

"It was an accident!"Ray shouted behind him, as Daniel started to chase him.

"I'll get you!"

"Noo!"

Big rock soup

The sweet smell of sawdust always seemed to linger in his flared nostrils. He always felt a keen sense of exhilaration as rough hewn wood morphed into something beautiful under his hands. There was no doubt that John-John loved his work, but it was definitely one of those evenings when the sight of a No. 11 ZR from Silver Sands to town – packed like a Brunswick tin of sardines – would be welcomed.

John-John Augustus Joseph had burnished skin like strong, freshly-brewed tea. Faded Tommy Hilfiger jeans rode low on his sinewy hips as he ambled down Enterprise Road, limp backpack slung over his left shoulder. Each step made the leather pouch threaded on a slender thong around his neck, bump against his broad chest.

Short nails on the callused fingers of his right hand scratched lightly at black waves sitting close to his head. It was just hair to him – compliments his Vincey father – but the girls in the village seemed to think it was something special – especially Blanda. She was a case!

He recalled their latest encounter on the weekend before.

Hands akimbo on broad hips below a tiny waist, her full, dark eyes (with breasts to match) followed his every move, from saw horse to compressor to electric saw, in the neat workshop nestled in his garden. Her tongue circled glossed, pouty lips in anticipation as she watched John-John's biceps bunch under his shirt as he planed a plank of mahogany. The sight of his hands clenching and moving sent a frisson of pleasure to arch along her spine. Petite Blanda loved to make sport and love with the same abandon. Later as Blanda stretched under John-John on his rumpled double divan, she often said he reminded her of some American singer, when she gently tugged at the two tiny gold hoops dancing in his ears. She hummed in tune with a sensuous R&B melody thumping on the radio. "JJ, you real sexy... just like Usher, onliest ting, black," she giggled.

Propping himself on his elbows, John-John's forehead furrowed as he frowned at her.

"Wuh you talkin'? Study it, we *all* black togedda!"

Blanda's ears grew hot and she bristled as John-John rolled on his back and emitted a long chupse at her intended praise.

Pelting a derisive glance his way, the young woman snatched up her sarong and flounced in the direction of the tiny bathroom at the back of the house. A long silence followed the door slamming.

I mean, she sporty, look gud and cuh handle sheself in de kitchen an' ting but not too rashole bright. I cyan' understand. It was nonsense like dat... dat is why Gran seh, 'Yuh should never got a woman unless she gots something wort'while between she ears.'

These days when John-John visited Blanda's bungalow about a mile from his house, Ernesta, her mother, as she swished around the kitchen would murmur, "Wif Cicely ovuh an' away, Earlene gone, is time enough dat anudda woman, a *wife*, should be hottin' pot fuh he." Blanda would simply dimple as she dished out a heaping plate of steaming kingfish and ground provisions on a large plate for him. Though Miss Brathwaite's "han' was sweet", somehow, the comments seemed to form aloe juice in his mouth.

Speaking of appetite, his stomach rumbled like an old motor boat under his forest green t-shirt. Some of his grandmother's *Sopa de pedra* with split peas and dumplings and chicken and poor man's pork, would go down easily now. He eased the blue haversack over the other shoulder. But the village was a two hour bus ride and walk away and payday was Friday. Well, it was Wednesday right now and his protesting belly didn't know the difference. Not that he didn't have money but John-John liked to recline quietly with his evening meal at home. Blanda would often tease that he was 'strange and cheap'. *Just because I don' really check for Chefette, KFC nor nuffin so...* but the fast food didn't wuk up on his palate the way his grandmother's (or even pushy Miss Brathwaite's) did.

Things were really different this year. It was a little slow at Ramnarine's Furniture Emporium right now. But then again, everybody knew January was the longest month of the year. With Christmas holidays over, nobody was really looking for anything. That is why John-John's orders dripped like molasses. However, he knew it was only for a time. Good thing he was frugal. Besides, he knew people that would offer him a little job work here and there. Plus, his reputation for timeliness and fine craftsmanship kept the work flowing.

Money really wasn't a problem; John-John believed in paying himself first with a hefty deposit at the City of Bridgetown Credit Union. Then he thriftily set something aside for groceries, bus fare and bills each week. John-John even budgeted for an occasional round of beers with the boys at Sammy's Shop. However, after ensuring that Gran was 'put down proper' and fixing up the little greenheart house she left him, John-John was even more reluctant to make unnecessary expenditure. He saw from the newspapers that the economy these days didn't look right.

Sopa de pedra. A waterfall sprung in his mouth at the very thought. He recalled Gran's cackling and the crinkling at the corners of her brown almond-shaped eyes that mirrored his. "Boy, long time ago before Cicely, you mudda, did born, I clap eyes 'pon you gran'fadda, Augustus, who you name fuh. He name mean 'worthy of respect', you know dat?"

Nodding, he *did* know but never tired of hearing.

Head tilted in that way of hers, she took a deep breath and continued.

"Well, he went tuh sea to nuff places like Panama and Enguland and Cape Verde Islands. Gussy did like it bad and mek nuff friends. He seh dat some Almeirim fellas did he good, good buddies from Portugal, yuh know. Dah is near tuh Spain. Anyhow, dese fellas nuses tuh mek *Sopa de pedra* – stone soup. Soun' funny, nuh? Gussy seh it taste real sweet doh. Well, he bring me back piece ah Portugal, faif! He seh, tuh show *me* how to mek it – Bimshire *Sopa de pedra!*" At this point usually her eyes would squinch up and the mirth would make her generous curves tremble. It was his cue to laugh along with her and he always obliged; their joy pealing sweetly to the rafters.

But last year at her bedside at Queen Elizabeth Hospital, she called to John-John to share his favourite love story, he suspected, for the last time. Her now frail body for the first time had that old people's smell that he couldn't stand, but he didn't care. He held her close anyway. John-John felt something hard and rough in his hand as Gran, gasping for breath, spun her *Sopa de pedra* tale in a whisper for the last time. When her spirit was released, it was his grandmother's Portuguese stone pressed in his hand.

Sopa de pedra.

The same trade winds that made the three coconut trees ahead shimmy, pushed the tendril of smoke John-John's way. His steps slowed just past Land's Down Road. Two fellas, Khiomal and Lintus, who usually limed around this time, were busy under the shade of a tamarind tree in a clearing in front of a pink-wall house to his right. Khiomal, the taller one, dark with blonde dreadlocks was scrutinising a good-sized breadfruit. Lintus, the shorter, brown-skinned, lithe youth sporting a moustache and neat cornrows, was fussing with a fire. A large buck pot with a lid rested nearby on a worn bench. They returned his nod and resumed their tasks.

"Man, is a perfect day fuh roas' breadfruit, men." John-John fingered the leather pouch at his throat, as the young men grunted their approval. "But *Sopa de pedra*... now dat is food, fuh real," he added closing his eyes, licking his full lips and resting one foot on an old oil drum nearby.

"Suh – who?"

"*So-pa de pe-dra*," John-John enunciated slowly. "Real sweet food, den. You know when you mek dis fuh a woman, she does follow you 'bout. Study it, dem does like it bad."

"Yeah?" Lintus raised his eyes as interest spread across his face. "But... wuh um is?"

"A soup boy, dah wuh mek a pitbull pop he chain. Look, I gine show wunna how Gran nuses to mek it. Wash out dah pot, right? An' put on some water fuh boil. An'... Khiomal, bring me a pot spoon and some salt. Weh de pipe to wash my hand?"

"It dey," indicated Khiomal pointing in the direction of the stand pipe. "Lintus boy, leh we see if dis gine help you get Belinda. I gine fuh de spoon." Khiomal, walking away, chuckled at Lintus' scowl.

In five minutes, Khiomal jogged up with the spoon in a wrinkled paper bag. By then, the water was bubbling in the large pot. John-John nodded and ceremoniously removed his grandmother's Portuguese stone from the pouch around his neck. After the *plops* of the stone into the gurgling water, John-John carefully sprinkled salt into the pot. Taking the large spoon, he slowly stirred. Ignoring the slack mouths of his assistants, John-John spooned a little of the hot liquid onto his open hand, closed his eyes, sucked his palm and smacked his lips. *Sopa de pedra, man.*

"You, like you mekkin' big rock soup, yeah," Lintus guffawed, recovering from his shock.

"Big rock wuh?" a contralto feminine voice queried. "So, who cookin'?"

Six eyes feasted on the belle of the village – Belinda Fingall. Sooty lashes framing large, hazel, kohl-rimmed eyes, brushed her high cheekbones. Artfully applied coral lip gloss glistened on a slightly-parted, full mouth. The purple tied dyed shift dress which hinted at the young woman's lush figure, exactly matched her flat leather sandals. A Super Centre shopping bag swung against the mocha-kissed skin of her shapely calves.

"I. *Sopa de pedra*. Is Portuguese." John-John reluctantly returned his attention to the simmering pot. "Hmmm… yeah. Could use lil onion an' a few split peas, doh."

Belinda, intrigued, reached into her plastic bag. "Oh, take one of mine. An' a couple cloves of garlic too."

"T'anks," smiled John-John taking the proffered offering from her slim hand. *She was sweet, boy.*

Lintus, shifting restlessly, harrumphed loudly, "Wuh nex'?"

At the tinkle of split peas crashing against the metal, John-John slowly considered. "Wunna got sweet potata?"

Khiomal got up from his crouched position near the fire. "I gine check my aunt. Wuh about we breadfruit?"

John-John nodded.

Belinda perched daintily in the shade on the worn bench. "Y'all gine put me in the pot?"

Lintus swallowed and snatched up the breadfruit and started peeling furiously and murmured, "Of course, baby."

Jean Scantlebury, who lived two houses down, set down an overflowing plastic basket of washing. The middle-aged woman was just about to step into her freshly swept verandah, when her suspicious eyes took in the activity by the tamarind tree.

"Wuh y'all up tuh?"

John-John, who was crouching, looked up at a short woman with a sweaty, creased face surrounded by a red bandana.

"Evenin' Miss Scantlebury. John-John mekkin' we a special soup," Belinda offered politely.

"Oh?" Staring at the young man warily, Scantlebury's brow furrowed.

By this time Lintus and Khiomal handed John-John the sliced breadfruit and sweet potato heaped in an enamel basin. Khiomal grinned like a Cheshire Cat as he proffered John-John a fresh sprig of broad leaf thyme. "My mudda sen' dis."

John-John nodded his approval as he took the herb from Khiomal. "Boy, now you talkin! Gran nuses tuh–"

Scantlebury sniffed appreciatively and interrupted, "Like wunna know 'bout soup. But wait, is ital soup or wuh? I knows you fellas might not want nuh pig tail but nuh chicken?"

John-John stood up and cocked his head. "You cuh spare some madam?"

Scantlebury impatiently said, "Yes, got a chicken dah done season up. Coming back now."

As she bustled off, Belinda stared at John-John, her eyebrows arched. "Well, well, well… Gypsy Scants cuh surprise you when she ready. John-John, yuh real good!"

Not to be left out of the warmth of Belinda's sunshine, Lintus abruptly stood up, dusted off the back of his jeans and started jogging towards Land's Down Road. Over his shoulder, the muscular youth shouted, "Joseph, I gine home to come back."

Belinda, looking bemused, smiled. She crossed her legs, leaned back and tossed her long braids.

Shortly the slip-slop of Scantlebury's yellow rubber slippers slapped against the tarmac.

"Come," she panted, handing the bowl of chicken to John-John. "Tek dese English potatas and dese carrots. You gine need some black pepper too." At Belinda's startled expression, she mumbled, "Dey duh getting ready to spoil, anyhow." Turning briskly towards her small house down the road, Scantlebury declared, "Holler fuh me when it done, hear?"

About thirty-five minutes later, the Portuguese stone wove more of its magic on the small hamlet. Some older men from the village set up a rickety wooden table nearby to play dominoes. A few children shrieking from a lively game of tag raced up and down the field in the molten light of the sunset. Scantlebury sauntered back with Miss Chandler, a slim, bespectacled older woman, who lived in the white chattel house near Chicken Rita's. Both were holding bowls. Another young woman, Sherissa, who was seated next to Belinda on the bench nudged her and uttered sotto voce: "Lynn, check the two ah dese!"

Miss Chandler, waving, called cheerfully, "Evenin! Y'all having a party? Young fella, you want dis?" slipping a clear plastic bag bearing fragrant marjoram and thyme, from the pocket of her apron.

"T'anks." John-John took it from her smiling.

John-John lifted the lid to add Miss Chandler's contribution to the pot. A collective sigh wafted from everyone that evening in the pasture at the glorious scent.

"Dah done now," asserted Scantlebury.

"Nah man!" rumbled a loud baritone.

It was Lintus, bearing a tea towel-covered enamel dish.

"Dumplings, man, wid corn meal, a bit ah nutmeg and lil coc'nut."

"Wuh?" Belinda and Sherissa chorused. "You mudda mek dem!"

Miss Chandler shook her head. "No love. I am his aunty. He cuh really mek dumplings."

Belinda's thoughtful stare made Lintus' hand tremble. "Huh," he growled pushing the dish in John-John's direction.

John-John added the dumplings one by one gently to the pot.

Sopa de pedra, man.

Tree frogs chirped, "It is time. It is time," from fragant khus khus on the field.

Everyone made a beeline for the simmering pot.

Scantlebury waited patiently at the head of the queue.

After John-John ladled a generous portion in Miss Scantlebury's dish, she held out a second bowl to him. "Dah is fuh you," she muttered gruffly. "It smell real good. Wuh is dah funny name you call it again?"

John-John beamed as the savoury fragrance of *Sopa de pedra* lingered in the air.

Under the poui

"Wait for me darlin', I'll come back for you!" he whispered as he rose dressing himself, brushing the few yellow poui that fell atop his exquisite chocolate body. The warmth of heartbreak filled my eyes and silent, salty beads flowed down my cheeks as I realised this would be our last day together for a long time to come.

"I will miss you Derrick," I said, between sobs.

"Oh gosh Nandi, don't cry, I'll come back, I promise!" he said as he buttoned up his white shirt. He looked so smart in white.

"Do you have to go for such a long time?"

"Well, becoming a doctor takes time. Besides I want to give you the best of everything and I can't do that if I don't have money!" he said with a half-crooked smile.

He handed me my dress – my favourite, short, purple strap dress – and I slipped it on slowly, prolonging the time before he would leave me to follow his dream.

"You're so beautiful, and you look so sexy in that dress!" he chuckled, as he pulled up my zipper and wiped my cheek with his soft hand.

"Make sure you call me!" I said.

"Of course I will!" he said. "Every week, I promise!"

He took me in his arms and pulled me against his body, embracing me so tightly that I felt a stimulating sizzle through my body; I wanted to make love to him again, merging us into everything that was one being. There was so much more than love and passion between us. The electricity was exhilarating. I knew I would definitely miss this connection – it was the first time I ever made love to someone, it felt so real to have that kind of passion and the 'feel good' feeling.

"Okay, I have to go now, I'm going to miss my flight and I'm sure dad is waiting for me."

He looked into my eyes for what seemed like a long time then kissed me feverishly on my lips.

"Goodbye Nandi. I… I love you!" he said as he picked up his backpack and walked away.

I watched him drive off till his dad's green Almera disappeared along the dusty road.

He said he loved me. It was the first time he ever said it, though I told him I loved him many times before. I was filled now with an astonishing joy, because I know now how he really felt and wanted to believe he would keep his promise and return to me one day. He would whisk me away from my monotonous life, away to a foreign country – I always dreamed of visiting, even living in England or the United States or even India. We would get married and raise a family together and he would help me further my education. *Ah yes, my life would change somehow!*

I laid down under the poui, gazing through the gorgeous flowers – almost glowing in the evening sun – daydreaming of what our house would look like, all the finery we would live in, because doctors earned lots of monies! I heard my mother call out to me from across the field, screaming at the top of her lungs.

"Nandi! Time to come home girl!"

I packed my belongings, straightened my hair and walked home feeling content now that I not only loved Derrick but was IN LOVE with him.

"I can't believe you were so careless!" mother yelled. "How could you have made such a mistake? I taught you better than that, child, I so disappointed in you, you so lucky your father not living to see this happen, he would've bury you alive!"

"I'm so sorry mom!" My tears burned my tired eyes. "He said he will come back, he promised!" I pleaded.

"It is October now, six months since he gone, not ah single phone call or letter and you still believe he coming back... FOR YOU?" she argued. "What you will do if he don't come back, eh? What? I tell you these ragamuffins 'round here only want one thing. Just because his mother and father nice doesn't mean he nice too!"

Her questions scared me, I never once thought about how his abandonment would affect my new situation. I wanted to believe that he was just busy with school but that was bullshit. Six months was too long to be *so* busy to not call your girlfriend who you had sex with for the first time!

I placed my hand on my tummy, wishing that I knew how to contact him, tell him that he would be a father and I needed him now more than ever. In that moment I missed him and hated him and loved him all at once. Mom stormed out of my room, slamming the door behind her.

It's been this way since we found out I was pregnant about two months ago; the quarrelling, sudden bursts of anger thrown against me, long nights of crying myself to sleep. I knew that was her way of dealing with my situation. I deserved every bit of resentment she showed me. I let her down and probably ruined my life. No school now, it was too late to have an abortion and besides that mother and I had both decided that an abortion was against our Hindu and personal beliefs.

She came back awhile later with a tray of food. She hugged and kissed me and apologised for her behaviour. I told her that I forgave her; she was just being a good mother! I ate wearily while we spoke about the Divali celebration that would be held in a couple weeks, ignoring for the moment my bulging tummy. We decided it best that I should not attend, even though the gossip was already spreading about my pregnancy and that Derrick had left me; everyone in this part of Moruga knew Derrick and I were dating.

My mother didn't approve of it but allowed me to make my own decisions about him. *Maybe it would have been better if she had ordered me not to see him, I might not have been in this position right now… PREGNANT! Oh! Shut up Nandi, the deed is done, now you have to live with the consequences.*

Mom's voice interrupted my internal babbling. "Well I think we should let his parents know what's going on. Ent they like you? They should be able to tell us why he not calling and maybe give you a number or address or something!"

"Sounds good but I not going there alone, you will come with me right?" I asked.

"Of course child, don't be stupid!" she smiled. *I really love my mother.* Then she told me to eat and get some sleep.

I couldn't sleep of course. My mind played out scenarios of what would happen when we would visit Mr. and Mrs. Phillips. Of course everyone would think that I was trying to blame it on Derrick because his family was wealthy and, well, my mother and I were 'getting by'. But Derrick's parents knew that he and I had been sweethearts throughout most of secondary school. He attended Presentation College in San Fernando, whilst I attended San Fernando Government Secondary School.

He was only one year older than me and we travelled together to and from school. He was in Lower Six when I wrote CXC last year. I decided to take a break before going back to school and he decided to finish his education (persuaded by his mother) in London.

Maybe they would be angry that he wasn't in contact with me. Or, maybe, they would believe the rumour that I was blackmailing them, saying the child was Derrick's and I wanted money. *Of course not!* In my opinion, they approved of us, even treated me like their own.

Well, whatever the outcome I would most definitely get in contact with Derrick because I was pregnant and he was the only one I'd been with. They knew my mom and even my dad, before he died some years ago. They knew we were a respectable family and that Derrick was the only boy I ever took interest in. So they would certainly be calling him up, bombarding him with questions.

I ate while the ramblings in my mind eased to thoughts of that day under the poui tree; the day we gave ourselves to each other. I looked out my window to the land filled with the skeletons of the poui trees no longer in bloom. They were so different now, seemingly echoing the hurt in my heart. The trees looked forsaken without their luminous yellow and pale pink flowers, as forsaken as I felt.

My father adored the trees, said it was the most ridiculously beautiful trees when in bloom. That's why he never left this rural part of the village. There were only two houses besides ours on this street. It was lonely, so lonely that the street wasn't ever paved. But we had water and electricity, so the road was no big deal. I missed my father, I knew he would have beaten me till I was blue for letting this happen, but he would have also made sure that Derrick accepted his responsibilities.

"Nan, you ready yet?" mom wailed from downstairs. It was Saturday and she had already called to make sure the Phillips were home.

"Yes, I'm coming! Give me two minutes!" I yelled back.

We walked all the way to Demerol Street, where the Phillips lived. It was a long but pleasant walk. This part of Moruga was much more settled and the villagers stood and gawked at me as mom and I strolled by.

"Good morning Devya," Mrs. Cooper called from her porch.

"Morning Carlene," mother replied and waved to her. Everyone knew my mother because everyone had known my father. He was a taxi driver in the area. At almost every home we passed, we were greeted by more staring and hellos, all hellos addressed to my mother of course.

It was almost eight o'clock when we got to the Phillips' house, an immense, modern concrete house with two levels and fully air-conditioned. It was apple white and fenced around, with a big front lawn and a huge garage, holding four cars and it still had place for storage. They also had a pool in the backyard.

If I were rich like them I would leave here, maybe live West Moorings! I thought to myself. I knew the reason they stayed in Moruga was because Mr. Phillips' parents lived two houses away and he wanted to stay close to them. Well that's what Derrick told me.

"Good morning Mrs. Singh… Nandi darling, how are you!" Janet Phillips said, looking at my bulging tummy.

"Call me Devya, and good morning to you too," mother replied. I only smiled wryly. I could see the agitation on her face; obviously my mother did not inform her of the reason for our visit. She led us into her home, motioning for us to sit in the dining room. She offered refreshments but we declined. Mom wasted no time!

"Well Janet I think you know why we're here," she said as she placed her hand on my tummy. I shifted a bit uneasily, manoeuvring my baby doll dress, trying not to let my 'big belly' show too much.

"Well I did hear the rumours, but Derrick said that he broke up with Nandi before he left Trinidad," Janet said, looking to me first then shifting her gaze to my mother.

"Where is Mr. Phillips?" I asked. I liked Derrick's father, he was kind and understanding, much more than his mother. "I thought he was also going to be here?" I assumed my mother thought the same. She swivelled on her seat, searching around for him.

"Gone fishing for the weekend," Janet replied. "Anyway, so you're trying to say that *that*" – she pointed to my stomach – "is Derrick's?"

"Yes of course! Whose else it could be, eh? He didn't break up with Nan, at least that's what he made her believe!" mom replied bitterly. She told me to explain what happened the day Derrick left; what we did and the things he told me. I did, feeling very ashamed at recalling the event out loud for both of them.

Janet stood up when I was finished. She appeared disgusted by what she heard and was undoubtedly fuming. She explained to us that Derrick already met someone in London and that she thought I was trying to blame her 'innocent' son for something I did with someone else. She even said that I was a manipulator and indecent and a liar.

My mother was furious and like a typical 'Trini' woman, she argued with Janet, telling all sorts of horrible things about the way she raised her son and the kind of mother she seemed to be. A few cuss words flew between them both and mom grabbed my wrist, jerking upward, and dragged me out the house behind her.

I was still crying when we got home. After that day we scarcely spoke of Derrick and his parents anymore and decided we would take care of my child on our own.

I looked into my son's eyes; sweet honey hazel, just like Derrick's. I cried knowing that he may never know his real father. I cried because the betrayal was too much. Niraj was almost three months old and he was the most beautiful, delicate baby I ever saw. He was looking at the yellow poui flowers over us that filled the tree, smiling... laughing and reaching out trying to touch them. In his smile, I suddenly felt happy and hopeful for our future together. I placed him on the sponge and laid beside him, staring up into the tree like I did so many times before, talking to him and playing with his hands and feet.

Suddenly, I heard his voice behind the tree. "Looks just as beautiful the last time I was here." Derrick came around the tree and stood in front of me with a bunch of purple-rimmed carnations in his hand. My heart raced, beating so hard I felt it in my throat. He gave me the flowers and sat down beside my… our baby.

"My mother told me you met someone, so I never called," he said. "I didn't know you were pregnant, I'm so sorry!" Tears filled his eyes and he reached out, taking my hand in his. He explained that his father was the one who told him the truth and that he should come back to Trinidad to finish his education and take care of his new 'family'. He said he was not speaking to his mother because apparently she thought he was too good for me and had decided to lie to both of us, trying to keep us apart.

It was hard to listen to everything he said. He claimed sleepless nights, picturing me with someone else, making it difficult to focus on his studies.

"You didn't know. It's okay now," I finally said, crying.

"Can I hold him?" he asked, looking lovingly towards his son.

"His name is Niraj and of course you could hold him!" I said.

"He is just as beautiful as you are, maybe more!" he chuckled. They looked good together. He looked like a father now, still young but more mature and capable to hold his own.

"I came back for you, for both of you… just like I promised," he said, pulling my gaze from his body to his eyes.

"My mother is going to kill you!" I blurted.

"My father and I spoke to her a couple days ago. We explained everything to her. She's still upset a bit but she understands and forgives me," he replied sombrely.

I was happy now that he was here, to stay. He was mine and he would take care of me, of us. He handed Niraj to me then took my other hand pulling me up to my feet.

"I know all the pain and anger you must have felt. I know you thought I fooled you, but I never meant for any of it to happen. My mother will suffer for this, for hurting us this way. I told her she won't be able to see you or our baby until we could forgive her." His honey hazel eyes burned with regret and anger, but then simmered to a glow, so deep and so rich that I felt my body turn jelly-like, but I held my ground.

Niraj pulled on my hair, gurgling.

"Derrick, it's alright, I got over it, mostly when I had Niraj. He filled the void you left," I replied.

"You see, that's the thing, I need that space again, I need you to make that space in your heart for me again Nandi!" he said as he fished in his front jeans pocket and pulled out a purple suede jewel box.

"You would always have my heart; you're my first love, my first lover, my best friend!" I said.

He opened the box, revealing an exquisite diamond ring. I swear if I wasn't holding Niraj, I would have fainted!

"Marry me?" he asked, hesitantly. He really thought I still hated him. I couldn't say anything.

"Nandi, please, marry me! I want to give you everything I said I would. I want to keep all my promises!" he pleaded with me. He looked miserable but hopeful.

"Yes!" I whispered. "Yes!" louder this time, tears of joy flooding my eyes.

He put the ring on my finger, hugged us, squeezing us in the tender, familiar embrace I'd longed for. And for the first time in more than a year, I felt the scorching, sweet taste of his kiss.

God Save the Queen

Vernon Carpenter was a man desperate for a rum and coke. Despite constantly swallowing, his throat remained as dry as the yellow grass of the savannah on which he stood. It was as though his mouth got fed up of giving him saliva and shut down production. Vernon needed the shot of alcohol not so much to quench his thirst but to quell the nerves residing deep in the pit of his huge stomach. Something just wasn't right. He could feel it. The air was playful and unfettered around everyone but him. He watched with dismay as the breeze danced the dress hats off pompous women, cheekily exposing dimpled thighs. It swept balloons and kites away from tiny, distracted hands.

Vernon put his hand to his cheek. He couldn't feel the breeze at all. Not one damn bit, he exclaimed audibly. In fact he could barely breathe. It was as though the air screeched to a halt just as it approached him; warded off by some invisible force field. He looked around slowly, and then spun around faster as though trying to catch an imaginary tail, immune to the nearby laughter his actions aroused. But all appeared to be well. It was a fine day under azure skies and blazing sun in the little colony. The Queen Consort was one year older and Germany hadn't long surrendered. I should be happy, Vernon thought miserably. He wondered if the foreboding feeling had anything to do with the ominous words of his mother that morning, a self-proclaimed 'seer' woman.

She'd insisted Helen, Vernon's wife, not attend the parade but didn't elaborate on the reasons why. Helen had scoffed at the warning, downplaying her mother-in-law's intuitions, arguing that pregnancy wasn't a sickness. At the time Vernon agreed with Helen but now, as he passed his sweaty palms constantly over his salt and pepper hair, he wondered. He watched as the crowd moved with a careless synchronicity to the sweet and sensible calypso rhythms.

As much as Vernon could almost taste the alcohol swirling about in his mouth, he bought himself a bottle of mauby and looked around for his wife. In the past his drinking would lead to fights that saw the nearest breakable item in Helen's reach smashed to smithereens. She was convinced that drinking caused Vernon to be less virile. They'd been trying to conceive for years and she was tired, cross and taking no chances. Even though he used to make fun of Helen's amateur perspectives on the science of fertility, her expanding stomach in the last eight months had shut him right up. It was only the second time in a decade she had conceived.

Vernon caught a glimpse of Helen in the crowd, dwarfed in her pale blue gabardine dress by a towering policeman polishing his trumpet. Helen, he mused, looked good enough to eat. Like the mangoes that hung in old Mrs Timothy's front yard. The kind that sent juice running down to his elbow and made him forget decorum as he tracked its flow back up with his tongue. Like old Mrs Timothy, Vernon knew his wife could get real mean if anyone tried to touch what was hers. As he began to make his way towards her, a young Negro boy, as if suddenly struck by a most profound thought, blocked his path.

"Wait. How old the Queen is today?" the boy asked Vernon loudly, his forehead creased as though he were problem-solving a complex mathematical equation. The boy looked around at the crowd, his palms facing the cloudless sky. "Forty? Fifty? Who know the answer?"

The crowd's silence indicated the irrelevance of the question and the presumption that the boy was mad. The closest most people ever got to the Queen were the few coins jingling away in their pockets.

Moments later, the boy, receiving no answer to his query, resumed his gyration to the music and the air, its proper degree of nonchalance. The atmosphere, however, was soon interrupted by the presence of a true royalist.

"God Save the Queen," he sang happily, intoxicating anyone in close proximity with each exhale. Drunk by default you call that, someone called out. The poor savannah groaned under the weight of these Johnny-come-lately colonial subjects. The royalist droned on:

Send her victorious!
Happy and glorious!
Long to reign over us!
God Save the Queen!

Vernon couldn't explain or suppress the irritation he felt at the unrestrained happiness of the people around him. He tried to dance but his legs felt leaden and he feared he looked awkward and ridiculous. Even the newly discharged patients from the nearby clinic, bandaged and delirious on medication, hobbled to the music with less effort than him.

He let out a sigh of relief as he saw Helen sashaying through the carnival crowd towards him, wearing one of those sweet smiles that could grant her anything she wished. Her belly, high, pointy and if old wives' tales were anything to go by, home to a baby boy, was like a flashlight in a thick fog. Now, Vernon often joked with her, she was the one in the house with the bigger belly.

But Vernon's sixth sense just wasn't letting up. As he embraced Helen, he felt his body shiver.

"What happen, V?" she asked. "Why you trembling? You catch a fever or what?"

"I'm alright. C'mon. Come and sit for a little while, darling," he said, urging her away from the crowd. Although Helen looked tired Vernon knew she would not submit easily.

"I didn't come here just to sit down," she said, extracting her elbow from the pinch of his grasp. "Soon I'll be sitting for longer than I care to. So just let me enjoy myself."

"Oh gosh, Helen, *please*. Just take it easy."

She shot Vernon a fiery look. One that, as soon as he received it, immediately made him hope it had accurately conveyed her feelings so that a soliloquy would not have to follow. Her expression wore the painful facts of a distant history so well that he contorted his face to let her know that, yes indeed, he'd got her point, and she need not bother herself to verbalise the issue. But for Vernon there was no such luck.

"Take it easy? Take it easy you say? You got pregnancy amnesia or what man? You forgot what happened last time? After I was so careful with everything and took it *so easy*?"

Vernon knew when it was best to shut his mouth. He averted her piercing, brown eyes and dutifully let her rebuke wash over him.

"Sorry," he said meekly. He wanted to say more but opted instead to study the various discolorations of his toenails as they protruded his sandals.

"I did everything perfectly last time," she said softly, taking his hand in hers. "And still, the Lord saw it fit to take it away. Perhaps if I just act normal this time, enjoy things and not worry too much, it'll come right you know?"

"Yes Helen, of course, sugar." He apologised a few more times. "Come, let's sit down a bit, right?"

They passed large aluminium pots of corn soup perched stoically on gas burners and barbeque chicken being smothered with sauce in open pits. Normally Vernon would devour these without a second's thought but that day his stomach rebelled and he stifled the needed to gag.

People made room for them on one of the wrought iron benches under a large *samaan* tree.

"You want a coconut water, sugar?" Vernon asked, rubbing the curve of Helen's lower back.

"Mmm." The sound barely left her lips as her eyes fluttered with pleasure.

Vernon motioned to the Indian boy, perched on his laden wooden cart, who deftly sliced the top off a medium-sized, yellow coconut with a perennial skill. Vernon kept staring at Helen, eagerly wiping away the trickles of coconut water that escaped her mouth. She gave him sporadic, suspicious looks but said nothing.

A few hours later, the energy of the crowd was palpable. Vernon knew it was only a matter of time before the euphoria of the day was replaced by a collective itching to start fighting in the streets. Nightfall in the city gave rise to phantom borders between good and evil, restraint and indulgence. But Helen paid little mind to Vernon's pleas, dragging him towards the sound of powerful drumming. It was a stick fight, an old African tradition of skilful combat between two opponents with long sticks made of *poui* wood. Vernon sucked his teeth. The intensity of the drumming could still wake the ancestors but they wouldn't find anything but a farcical shadow of a former great art. It usually ended only when first blood flowed from the head of one of the contenders. Vernon knew it was no place for Helen.

But she moved her body seductively to the drumming, sticking out her behind and shuffling back. She laughed as she threw her hands in the air, revealing a few black hairs under her arms. Vernon succumbed to the smile he felt was taking shape. It was like watching his wife for the first time.

Just then the crowd swelled out slightly as a stick fighter raised his stick in a mock gesture, before stamping his foot, executing a pseudo African dance movement and provoking his opponent to strike. Helen didn't move quickly enough as the crowd heaved and someone stepped on one of her rubber slippers. She struggled to free herself and Vernon rushed to her side. He felt like he'd flirted enough with fate.

"Helen, it's time to go."

This time she didn't protest. She rubbed the sweat off her forehead with the back of her hand and looked at him mischievously, as though she'd gotten away with far more than she'd expected to.

"You worry too much, you know that?" Helen said as she linked her arm into Vernon's. She was leaning on him more than usual, dragging her burst slipper and yelping occasionally as her skin touched the burning road.

The tram was in sight. Vernon smiled as though he'd outwitted life itself. The mind is a tricky bastard, he thought. He felt his shoulders slump a little.

As they walked, a small crowd of little revellers, barely three feet tall, walked towards them. One little girl, no more than six years old and the possible product of a bored American soldier and a wide-eyed island girl, stopped and placed her hand on Helen's stomach.

"Is it a girl?"

"Ah, I don't know," Helen said, clearly unprepared for this medley of personal space invasion and childhood innocence.

"What are you going to name him?"

"What?"

"You should call him Job."

"I told you, we don't know if it's a boy yet." Helen gave Vernon a quizzical look. The little girl's hand was still on Helen's belly.

"Okay, go on now," Vernon said to the girl, nudging Helen along. "Stay with your group."

The youngster stared at Vernon, her hazel eyes challenging his with unabated intensity. The two craned their necks to hold the gazes, until the little girl looked away and ran ahead to meet her friends. Vernon was disturbed. But when he looked back, the girl, skipping happily, appeared to be taking no further notice of them. Helen was going on about the precociousness of children nowadays when she noticed something on the road.

"Is that a lucky penny over there?" she asked.

She unlinked her arm and he immediately felt a gush of cold air envelop his back and under his arms, causing his body hairs to stand to attention. Vernon felt anxious but instead of his heart racing, it seemed to slow down. Every thump felt like a painful squeeze that ended in an echo all around him.

"Sugar, I'm just going to check they have a seat for you." Vernon ran ahead as Helen walked towards the coin.

When he got to the tram he looked back. Helen was still crouched down. Does it take that long to pick up a penny? he thought. Well she always bit her nails. Even after they hurt and bled, she still bit them. He kept telling her that bitten nails were unsightly and looked unhygienic. But did she listen to him? People with short nails can't pick up coins off the street very quickly now can they?

The tram was getting ready to go. Helen still hadn't stood up. They were cheap rubber slippers anyway, Vernon told himself. He remembered always telling her "good things not cheap, and cheap ting eh good." But did she listen to me? Now she had to spend a few moments fixing her slipper so her feet wouldn't burn.

Get up Helen, he whispered, get up, my love. The air, which had previously eluded him so skilfully, was now blowing directly into his face, shooting up into his nose and settling in the open spaces of his brain. He began running frantically towards her.

"Helen!" Vernon shouted. "Helen!"

Her face was frozen with pain. Her left hand cradled her stomach. The coin remained untouched.

"Helen, what happened?" His question went unanswered as Helen kept calling out for the Lord.

The waiting room of the nearby clinic was full of self-inflicted casualties, drunks and troublemakers, prima donnas with heat exhaustion and careless revellers oblivious of broken glass and nails.

"Where's the doctor?" Vernon shouted to a nurse as he gingerly placed Helen on a chair.

"You have to wait," she said, barely looking up. "Fill out these forms and take a seat."

"Please, she lost a baby before."

"The doctor will see her as soon as he can."

Helen was sweating profusely and squeezing Vernon's hand. She'd barely spoken, preferring to stare intently into his eyes, except when the pain caused her to arch her head back and squeeze her eyes shut. Vernon couldn't meet her gaze for too long but instead cradled her head, occasionally blowing on the back of her neck. People looked at him with sorrowful eyes, demoting the importance of their own afflictions with every stare.

"Where's the doctor!" Vernon screamed. But instead of staff rushing to his aid, the waiting room merely constricted for a few seconds after his outburst and then relaxed again. It was a national holiday, few doctors were in and there was nothing else to do but practise patience.

Then there was a thud. Helen's body jerked and shuddered involuntarily. This time the nurses rushed to her and three of them carried her into the theatre. Vernon looked around as though in a daze. He saw people speaking, their mouths contorting into countless, unnamed shapes, but couldn't hear any of the words escaping their lips.

He stared out the window at the dark night for what seemed like hours later, and then, without prompting, turned around towards the nurses' station. A weary doctor chatted silently to a nurse. Vernon watched them look around the room before quickly lowering his eyes to the floor, his weary body cutting a sorrowful, prayerful pose. He hoped that this would somehow cocoon him against any bad news. But when he looked up he saw the nurse's hand slowly ascending, a taut index finger attached, pointing directly at him like a poisoned arrow. The doctor's eyes were barely able to conceal defeat.

Vernon stumbled out of the clinic, welcoming the assault of the cool air and the aimless dust from a near-empty savannah. He blinked through the wall of water his face had become. Somewhere in the distant night, the faint and tuneless royalist's encore of "God Save the Queen" wafted slowly towards him and, in dramatic irony, fell at his feet.

The Winged Girl

The rays of the moonlight penetrated Jesse's room. Half asleep, she seemed to manipulate the shadows on her wall into ghoulish figures and ghastly creatures. This was her attempt to drift off into her own little wonder universe, where anything was possible. She had often dreamt about various fantasy worlds and different time zones, but every night, The Winged Girl would slip into her dreams and take her on the most magnificent ride of her life. Deep inside her heart, Jesse knew to herself that The Winged Girl was a reality.

Jesse's fifteenth birthday was only days away. She seldom thought about turning fifteen, but repeatedly about the trip to the family's beach house on Marine Bay to celebrate it. Every year, the Morgans took this sacred visit to the bay for Jesse's birthday; it was her priceless retreat. Somehow, the beach proved to be a serene location where she could let loose and let her emotions and power of invention run amok. This was the weekend she waited so patiently for, and Marine Bay was the place The Winged Girl proved genuine existence to her.

On the much anticipated day, Jesse was already packed and waiting. Her brown leather suitcase lay across the wooden floor of her bedroom, almost blending in with the unvarnished strips of wood. She desperately looked around her room in an attempt to find something she forgot to pack. Rummaging through her mahogany chest of drawers, she found a sketchpad. It was old and soiled, and flipping through it she saw years of familiar sketches and drawings from previous visits to Marine Bay. This was the only thing she really needed to survive the weekend. While reminiscing, she heard the sound of her mother's voice, sharp and full of vigour:

"Let's go dear!"

Jesse looked at herself in the mirror. Ringlets of dense auburn hair was pulled back into a bushy pony tail; piercing, brown eyes lay under thick, well-arched eyebrows, and full pink lips was what she saw. Gazing at herself she said: "This is it!" Her enthusiasm made her heart skip a beat or two as she hurried downstairs.

The journey was just as she expected it to be; long, boring and full of conversations with her parents about school and her future, not something she wanted to talk about at that particular time. Sometimes she accidentally zoned off into a daydream while her parents were busily chatting with her, and then simply smiled and nodded at them to show her 'keen interest'.

"Finally!" Jesse screamed as they pulled into the driveway of the beach house. It looked the same to her, just a bit older and dirtier. The driveway was made out of pebbles that her father found on the north side of the beach. There were truck-fulls of them on that part of the shore. The house itself was a wooden structure with glass window panes that possessed a thick film of dirt and grime. The galvanised roof was unpainted and often sprung a leak or two when it rained, and her father built a wooden deck all around the house, by himself. It was pretty extensive and entertained many moonlit nights on the beach. On entering the house, it smelt of old, musty furniture, and encompassed loads of dust particles that seemed to swim through the damp air. Jesse was discouraged. Was this her private retreat that she was so eager to indulge in? Despite the uninviting facets of the house, she was persistent to divert her disgust and repulsion, towards the main initiative for her being there, The Winged Girl, and her birthday of course.

The comforting scent of fresh coffee brewing made Jesse's eyes pop open at 6:03 A.M.. Wrapped up in a red fleece blanket, she trotted downstairs and into the kitchen. "Good morning mom, good morning dad," she croaked. Her parents were shocked to see their daughter up so early, but Jesse had planned every waking moment of her weekend and was not going to lose precious time sleeping unnecessarily. She took her steaming coffee and sketchpad with her onto the front deck. She loved illustrating, especially the outdoors. As she sipped and savoured every bit of flavour, her eyes wandered and gazed ahead. What a striking sight. The ocean was calm and a light mist hovered over. Rays of sunlight squeezed its way through the thick clouds, casting pink and orange ribbons that floated through the sky. The air itself was clean and crisp, and the tender current of soft breeze that brushed her cheeks was slightly chilled. "Today is going to be a great day," she said, as she picked up her pencil.

Jesse stood there for awhile admiring the picturesque scene right before her eyes. The mist started to diminish, the clouds dispersed and the sun shone in all its radiance. Waves tumbled toward the shore in ten second intervals and the metallic, emerald, green water never seemed more inviting. But something caught the corner of her eye. A figure appeared to be floating in the distance, a human figure. She dropped her coffee mug, watched it shatter, and ran towards the beach, her feet pounding on the loose, shell-laden sand. She knew what it was; she knew who it was.

She tried so hard to see beyond the glittering sea, her eyes squinted and teary. This was not the first time she experienced this mystifying occurrence. Jesse felt her body start to tremble with anticipation. Breathing heavily, she dropped on her knees, still following the figure with her eyes that could not seem to open wider than a grain of sand. Slowly the strange shape drifted closer and closer. Jesse often lost sight of it, but frantically regained focus. It was finally a few feet away from her. She stood up gradually, firmly planted her feet into the sand and clenched her toes tightly. Her thick, lengthy, ginger spirals blew across her face preventing her from seeing clearly ahead; maybe that was what she wanted, for she was so afraid yet so enthusiastic, she did not know which emotion to indulge.

Suddenly, Jesse witnessed the floating outline start to move. It elevated up and out of the water and stood on the shore. Jesse smiled. This was the moment she waited so restlessly for. A tall young woman faced her. Her pale skin seemed somewhat translucent and her hair was like the waves of the ocean, except golden. The tone of her eyes was tranquil but the intensity they had made Jesse intimidated. Her attire was breathtaking; a simple, flowing gown made out of white satin, embellished with pearls and shimmery fabric, and a silver tiara adorned the top of her luscious tresses. She looked angelic even though she was drenched and barefoot.

Jesse's heart leapt for joy as she stared at this girl. She looked the same as the last time she saw her. She looked the same in her dreams. This was The Winged Girl. But where were her wings?

"Where are your wings?" Jesse asked timidly.

The girl never answered. But instead, from behind her, out came two, magnificent, powerful things. They were a bit lucid with a hint of pink, and seemed to be magically glistening in the morning sun.

Jesse stared in amazement as the wings fluttered in the wind. She appears to be some sort of human butterfly, Jesse thought to herself. No one was around, the beach was empty. Even her parents were inside; they had no clue of what was taking place on the shore in front of their house.

"I have come to take you to a faraway land," said The Winged Girl. After all these years and visitations, Jesse never knew her name, she never asked. She contemplated for a while and decided she needed to know with whom she was speaking.

"May I, may I ask your name?" Jesse stammered.

She answered, "My name is Aldara, a winged gift."

How appropriate, Jesse thought to herself. They stood on the shore for quite some time. Aldara explained that she was a messenger sent from a different land. Jesse was attentive throughout this entire discussion. It was her first time speaking with The Winged Girl. She spoke a different tongue, but Jesse strangely understood every word.

Aldara took Jesse's hand and clasped it tightly. "Close your eyes," she whispered.

Jesse did as she was told, for she trusted Aldara, and in a matter of seconds felt a gust of wind envelop her body. Her nerves got the best of her, but she somehow managed to stay composed. She attempted to open her eyes but they were sealed shut.

"When the time is right," Aldara said with a reassuring voice.

Jesse still held on for dear life. She felt a sense of serenity and calm, a feeling that was bizarre to her. The next time she attempted to open her eyes, they released from their tight clinch.

A rich, green, lush meadow, with flowers and shrubs over-flowing tall lavish trees, surrounded her. Her feet were securely resting on the thriving grass, while her toes fiddled around. She stared in awe at the sight before her. It was enchanting. The air smelt of lavender with traces of a newly picked rose. Jesse never smelt anything like it, it automatically altered her mood. She imagined what it would be like to live here. Then, she immediately thought of her parents. What if they were out looking for her? She thought of their reaction when they realised she was nowhere to be found. She did not even know how long her stay would be at the magnificent new land. She wished that she would soon be home, for her parents' sake.

"What is this place?" Jesse asked Aldara, "It's so perfect!"

Aldara just looked at her and smiled.

Indeed, this place was perfect. Everything about the site was what Jesse's dreams were made of. She realised this when she saw a tree; long, slender branches with heart-shaped leaves of rainbow colours, dark brown trunk, and three, perfectly-positioned toadstools at the front of the base. She stared in awe. This was the tree in her dreams. This was the place she dreamt of night after night. Jesse wondered where she was. She constantly looked around but only saw greenery and flowering shrubs. No one else was there, it was remote, and it was a paradise. Aldara took her hand and walked throughout the fields. Jesse enjoyed this little talk and practically soaked up every bit of knowledge about Aldara. Jesse stared at her while they spoke, mesmerised. Aldara never mentioned to her where they were. Soon enough, Aldara informed Jesse that it was time to go home, but only to tell her parents an important message.

Jesse asked her, "Why can't I go home to stay? And what do I have to tell my parents? I don't have any message to deliver to them!"

Aldara notified her that she did have a message to convey, whether she liked it or not. Jesse was baffled; she just wanted to go home to her mom and dad. Aldara told her one more time, "Take my hand." She felt the sudden breath of air surround her once more and unsurprisingly could not open her eyes.

Jesse felt her feet land on sand. She opened her eyes and saw the beach, the shore, and her parents' house. She felt relieved and comforted to be home. She glanced around to find Aldara, but she was gone without a trace. She sat on the coast and thought of what happened. It was like a dream but more realistic, more tangible. She could see that it was late evening and the sun was not too far from setting. The tide was low and countless shells, rocks and strange objects of the sea were visible. Jesse walked toward her house.

"Where have you been young lady?" her mother shouted. "Don't you know the time?"

Jesse did not know what to say. She felt badly about the whole situation. She thought to herself that she should not have gone with Aldara; because of that, her parents were furious. "I just went for a stroll and I guess I lost track of the time. Sorry," she whimpered. Her parents did not say a word, but they understood. Jesse proceeded to help her mother prepare dinner.

While washing the dinner dishes, Jesse felt a presence behind her. She swiftly spun around. It was Aldara. Jesse felt her body go numb with shock and a bit of fright, for her parents were sitting right behind her.

"Don't you be anxious, they cannot see me," Aldara whispered.

Jesse did not know if to respond or just ignore; how would her parents react to her talking to herself? She overlooked the fact that Aldara was right next to her, and continued scrubbing dishes.

"Now is the moment. You have to address your parents now," Aldara declared.

Jesse was confused; she had no idea of what she was to say. After a few minutes of listening to Aldara, Jesse finally got the point of what was happening, or in fact, what was about to happen.

With tears in her eyes, she turned to her parents. They looked at her with concern and asked what was wrong. Jesse could not breathe, much less speak. She started to sob uncontrollably. Her parents quickly surrounded and tried to console her. She pushed them off and wiped her tears. She knew she had to be brave, she knew what she had to say to them. It was going to be the most difficult thing she ever had to say to anyone.

"I am going to a faraway land for good!" Jessed screamed. Her mother and father laughed, they had no idea of what was taking place and thought Jesse's hormones were probably getting the best of her. Jesse stayed calm and told her parents, "Stop laughing, this is serious. I needed to tell you, I needed you to know that I would no longer be here with you all. A girl named Aldara took me to a place today. It was the most spectacular sight I ever saw. It was magical, she was magical. It is my destiny to leave here and live my life there. I do not have a choice." Her parents still thought she was either lying or overreacting. Jesse hugged her parents tightly then went up to her room. She spent awhile there, preparing herself for what was to happen, and then she tiptoed out onto the beach. It was pitch black and the wind howled in her ear. Although she could not see the ocean, the salty smell could not go unnoticed. She felt tense; cleared her throat and took an infinite breath of hope.

"Are you happy now?" she yelled.

Aldara appeared to her and said, "Yes dear, I am happy and you should be too. This is your destiny; this was the plan all along. It was my duty to be here with you on this day; it was my task to take you with me. You should be elated."

Jesse was an emotional wreck. Her tears leaked down her face and soaked the front of her t-shirt. She replied, "If this is my fate, then I accept it."

Once again, they clasped hands and Jesse's eyes sealed shut. When they reached their destination, Jesse noticed that the sun was still out and it was broad daylight. How strange, she thought to herself. "I trusted you Aldara, now, what is my purpose for being here? I gave up my whole life, everything to be here," Jesse said with a calm voice.

"You are where you belong now. Do not be apprehensive, everything is as it supposed to be," Aldara reassured her.

"You brought me here, now tell me, where is this place? What is it called? I deserve to know!" Jesse said with a stern voice.

Aldara replied, "It was your time my child. This is Heaven."

Village story

Good day to you, one and all. Having a pleasant day? Well, you must be wondering why I in such a good mood. So, let me tell you. I was just remembering meh days in the village, and how things used to be then, long, long ago, and I thought you might like to hear about it. Life back then always had a little action, drama and all the works. So sit back, relax, and enjoy the story I am about to tell you. It might lift your spirits and put you in a good mood and remind yuh self of the life you living better than others.

First of all, let me introduce meself. My name is Martha St. Louis and I am from the village of La Brea. Now, I don't know if you ever hear 'bout this village, but in case nah, let me tell yuh, it is the home of the Pitch Lake. If you don't know 'bout the Pitch Lake then da is your problem. Look it up on the net nah. I doh have time to explain. I need to get on wid me story. But before I start the story, let me tell you, I narrating this story and I playing all the parts. What I say dey say is what dey really say, right? And I go play it out for you in a act. To make it more interesting nah. Understand? So let we begin the story:

Mavis: Martha! Martha!

Martha: Yes neighbour. What goin on wid you? Come in.

Mavis: Girl, you wouldn't believe the news I have for you. First, let me start wid Laura daughter.

Martha: What happen wid she?

Mavis: Wait nuh chile. Hmm, yes. Laura daughter, the big one, Peggy, she get big scholarship and thing girl. I hear she goin to University and thing soon.

Martha: A-a! Look how the chile get big nuh. Congrats and thing to she. But talk fast nah. What is the other news?

Mavis: Well, I hear the government letting foreigners come to Trinidad to work on we oil and gas sector.

Martha: No. I doh believe it.

Mavis: Wait, wait. Dat is not all. Hear what else dey doin. You see Susie husband Kenrick. Well you know he have big job and thing with LNG down Point Fortin.

Martha: Oh gosh! Doh tell me. He get the pink slip?

Mavis: Mhmm.

Martha: But why?

Mavis: Well, dey say dey didn't need him anymore. I don't know what he was working dey as, but I guess he wasn't important dey no more.

Martha: Oh gosh! I sorry to hear that. But how Susie goin?

Mavis: She dey. Yuh know she not working so I don't know how dey goin to make out. Kenrick go have to look for a job.

Martha: Yes, yes. And Susie go have to find a job too 'cause the money mightn't be enough. Steups, is hard times these days eh? Hard times.

Mavis: Yes girl, I know. Anyway, let me look to go home.

Martha: Yea girl, see yuh eh.

Mavis: Yea, I gone.

Martha watched as Mavis slowly made her way down the stairs and out into the night. She sighed as she walked back inside the house and soon began to busy herself with some clothes that needed folding. It was not long though that she had another visitor.

Lennard: Miss Martha. Miss Martha.

Martha: Like everybody calling to me tonight. Who is it?

Lennard: Is Lennard.

Martha opened the door to see a rather troubled boy.

Martha: What is it boy? Have a seat and talk to meh. Yuh want something to drink?

Lennard: Nah Miss Martha, is okay. I not staying long. But thanks eh. I looking for Sharon. Yuh see her today?

Martha: No, no. To tell you the truth I ain't see her in awhile. What happen, something wrong wid she?

Lennard: Miss Martha. I don't know what happen nah. All of a sudden is like I don't know she anymore. She not calling, not talking to me no more. And I could never seem to find her nowhere. Is like she hiding. 'Cause every time I ask one of she friends, they telling meh a different story. All kind of thing dey making up and saying, Miss Martha. I don't know what to do again nah, I don't know.

Martha thought to herself. She did know about Sharon. Yes. Most women in the village did know. But nobody wanted to tell Lennard for fear of terribly breaking his heart. She didn't want to have to be the one to tell him. How could she tell him that Sharon married a white man from San Fernando and gone to live in the big house with his mother? No. It was not time yet for him to know. Yes. That's right. She would wait for him to move on and then someone would break the news to him. But the rate he goin it go be a long wait.

Martha: Seriously, son, things does happen for a reason. Sometimes is because God don't want something to happen to you so he does do things to prevent some things from happenin. Yuh understand?

Lennard: Miss Martha, how it sounding like yuh trying to hint something to meh? Like you hear something 'bout Sharon?

Martha: No, no. But yuh missing the point I trying to tell yuh. Don't keep it on yuh mind too much. I am sure she is alright and, whatever happens, just remember things happen for a reason.

Lennard: Alright Miss Martha. I go try to remember. Yuh is a good woman. Thanks for the talk.

Martha: No problem son, is okay. Hurry along home now. Yuh say yuh wasn't staying long. Now look at yuh warming up me steps. Hurry along now.

Martha watched as Lennard exited the yard. He turned around to wave at her and shout goodnight. She waved back, then turned and walked back inside.

Martha: He's a good boy yuh know, a good boy. In time he go figure it out and understand, but for now, I think he should live his life not knowing. Girls these days is plenty a trouble. Dey primp and feisty and wutliss. But what yuh go do wid dem, yes. Blame it on the parents. Anyway, is not really my business.

Martha took her clothes upstairs and looked at the time. It was late and she already had had a long day. She needed her rest and tomorrow God spared would be another day.

Early the next morning, the village is alive with the sounds of women and children coming out to greet each other and men busying themselves with work and other doings in the yard. Louise is walking down the street and sees Susie in her yard. She turns to say hello.

Louise: Good morning, Susie! Goin down to market dis fine Saturday mornin?

Susie: No, I'm afraid not.

Louise: What happen chile? Something wrong?

Susie: Well, yuh know how dey layoff Kenrick from he job?

Louise: Oh gosh! No, I didn't hear! I sorry, but continue on.

Susie: Well, since dey lay him off, he ain't find no job yet. It kind a hard to find a job these days. Yuh know somewhere he could get a job?

Louise: Hmm... well, let me see. Umm, I think the construction site in San Fernando want workers, yuh know. I did see a sign. Yuh know whey dey have the big building goin up? Dey say dey need workers to do something, but girl I telling the truth I don't really remember what the job is but, umm, still find out nah.

Susie: Yes, thanks girl. Thanks a lot. Yuh don't know how much yuh help meh dey nah. But thanks a lot.

Louise: Is alright, girl. Have a blessed one.

Susie: Yes, yes same to you. And may the Lord bless your heart.

Susie went about her morning in higher spirits than she started off. And at the first chance she got, she told her husband about the job opportunity. He immediately went off in search of the contractor in charge and not much later, he was talking and negotiating about the job. Whether or not he got the job, that would be found out later.

In the market a villager vendor is heard shouting, "Sweet peppers, dollar a pound. Carrots, ten dollars a bag. Mango for the children, five dollars a heap." Everybody is bustling along getting the best prices for their market goods. While Martha is in line waiting to get her fish, she bounces up one of her long-time friends.

Martha: Oh, hello Mr. Thomas. Long time no see.

Mr. Thomas: Ah, my darling. How are you? You look fine as always. How's everything?

Martha: I'm good, good. And you Mr. Thomas? How you doing?

Mr. Thomas: I'm good, I guess I can't complain.

Martha: Well I haven't seen much of you around the village. Haven't been on your side lately. What you been up to?

Mr. Thomas: Well, I got meself a little job in Port of Spain, working as a bus driver for dem new buses the government providing. Yuh know the ones goin from San Fernando to Port of Spain and back.

Martha: Yes, yes. So you one a dem big drivers now? A-a! Congrats, congrats.

Mr. Thomas: Well thanks, eh darling. Nice seeing you again honey, but I must be on meh way.

Martha: Alright then, Mr. Thomas. See yuh.

After Mr. Thomas left, Martha continued collecting her market goods. While all was well for some on that side of the village, things weren't so well for others. Lennard, singing a dainty tune as he made his way to work, yippy tay yayyy… yippy tay yooo… I snap ma fingers I count to three… lose your pride and come dance wid me… yippy tay yayyy… yippy tay yooo…

As he reach and entered the yard where he worked, one of his co-workers brought him a message that the foreman on the job was here at the work and was expecting them to assemble for a meeting. He shrugged and made his way over to the assembled group. In the midst of the meeting, there was a knock on the door.

Clerk: Excuse me, but Mr. Foreman, a Sharon Henderson is here to see you.

Lennard jumped at the mention of the name Sharon.

Mr. Henderson: Oh, my wife is here to see me. Excuse me please, fellows.

Lennard wondered if it was just sheer coincidence that the foreman's wife's name was Sharon. It sure had made him jumpy hearing the name. He decided to take the time while the foreman was busy to get a drink of water. As he made his way to the fountain to get a drink, he got a glimpse of the foreman and his wife through the opened door. The fore-

man had forgotten to close the door behind him and in so doing had triggered a problem. For what Lennard saw was the woman he once used to spend lots of time with, in the arms of the foreman. Lennard stood there frozen in his tracks and very much soundproof of all the whispering that was being done by his co-workers. It had never occurred to him that she had married someone and had a new life of her own. He had just begun to believe that she had a very reasonable explanation for her sudden disappearance. Now, all that would have to be forgotten. By this time, Sharon had turned around and found Lennard staring at her. She awkwardly stood there finding it difficult to take her eyes off his sorry sight. Mr. Henderson, completely oblivious to what was goin on, was still talking, unaware of his wife's mood change. Lennard turned around, picked up his things and stormed straight out the door and out the gate. He didn't even stop to say anything to the guard and it was obvious by the way he had his face that he didn't want to be stopped either. He took a maxi straight down to La Brea, all the while calming down as he got closer to home. Without giving into any thought, he made his way straight over to Martha's house. He would talk to her and she would at least keep him from committing murder. He was that pissed. He called, his voice close to breaking for at this point he was almost in tears.

Lennard: Miss Martha!

Martha: Yes, what is it? *(She responded as she made her way outside to see who was calling.)*

Lennard: It's Lennard again. May I come in?

Martha: Sure, sure. Do come in. *(She was startled at the sight of the sorrowful boy.)* My, what happened wid you?

Lennard: Miss Martha *(crying now)* I find she wid the foreman. I didn't know. How she could do dis? I ain't do nothing to she. Why, Miss Martha, why?

Martha was troubled.

Martha: Who you talking 'bout boy? Sharon?

Lennard: Yes, Miss Martha. She wid the foreman. My foreman! She is he wife.

Martha: Oh God have mercy!

Martha was horrified. She knew the young wretch had gone and leave to marry a white man, but the poor boy's foreman? The cruelty of the girls these days was unbelievable. Lennard had found out and now he had come to her in a state and expecting to be comforted. What was she to do? She decided to play it slow, steady, easy.

Martha: Hush, hush now boy, mustn't let a woman see you cry like that.

Lennard: It doh matter now Miss Martha. I doh care who see.

Martha: Now, now don't say that. It's not the end of the world you know. Sure she gone and do this to yuh and I don't blame you for being sad, but yuh have to move on. When things like this happen yuh can't let people like that hold yuh back from moving on. Life too short for that. I'm sure that God have something good planned for you and that this is just a test to see how strong you are boy. I know yuh stronger than that. You is a man.

Lennard: But men does cry too.

Martha: Yes boy, men does cry too 'cause they only human, but they must never weaken they heart for long. Keep strong and move on boy, things does happen for a reason.

Lennard: *(Drying his eyes now.)* Yes Miss Martha. I hear you. But Miss Martha, tell me, you did know 'bout Sharon before? Did you?

Martha: Ha, ha. Well, yes boy. I did know she had gone to marry someone but I didn't know it was your foreman. But, you tell me now, how you figure me out?

Lennard: Well I did remember what you was telling meh before about how things does happen for reason And it was sounding, especially now, like you was preparing meh for something and like you did know what was going on, Miss Martha.

Martha: Ah, you is a smart boy, Lennard, a smart boy. Come on, think about it now. You know now that you deserve better than that, do you?

Lennard: Yes, Miss Martha. 'Cause if she didn't do it now she might o' do it sometime later.

Martha: Yes boy, you a smart one. Come have a drink wid me. Let us celebrate. For this one sacrifice of this girl greater shall be your reward.

And with that Martha and Lennard drank and were merry as they forgot the troubles of the wretched girl. Life was not always great but when sacrifices were made greater was the reward.

Tears for my mother

My father died when I was six. At least that is what I was told. My mother never talked about him and if I asked about him she'd whack me with whatever was handy – a fly swatter, a spatula, a hairbrush or sometimes she used her hand. I was nine the last time I was stupid enough to mention my dad. I remember it well because it was my birthday. My classmate Nellie's birthday was the week before and she'd had a party. I didn't go of course, my mother said that I looked like a ragamuffin and would be the laughing stock at the party. It had never bothered me before that my clothes were not pretty but when she mentioned it my attention was drawn to my sorry state. Since my father died I never got a lot of things. Come to think of it I never got anything new until the present one was outgrown or faded or tattered yet my mother was always dressing up and going out. She never took me with her. I stayed home alone, the television my only companion.

On the morning of my ninth birthday I awoke early, feeling for the umpteenth time that this day would be different.

That my mother would do something special for me, like bake a cake or surprise me with a present like she used to when daddy was alive. By afternoon when I saw nothing forthcoming, I approached her timidly, sensible enough to make sure there were no harmful objects around but still innocent enough to be hopeful. I don't know what made me feel that things would be different that day but I just couldn't help myself.

"Mom," I began and tried to gauge from her eyes what frame of mind she was in. It wasn't always bad. "Didn't daddy leave us money in the bank when he died? My teacher says that some people have insurance to protect their families."

At first she didn't say anything, just looked at me fixedly for a moment and then she jumped on me and screamed like a banshee, pulling my hair all the while. The attack was so sudden and so violent that I think I blacked out. When I came to she was sitting on a chair rocking backward and forward with a wild look on her face. She remained like that for hours till I could stand it no more and went outside to play.

We lived on the top floor of a three-storied apartment building which was owned by an old wrinkled woman of indeterminate age and ethnic origin. She spent every waking hour sitting at a small desk in the entrance hall of the building observing the comings and goings of the tenants. She knew everybody's business but her life was a closed book. Except for her name which was Jessie no one knew anything about her, where she came from or whether she had relatives or not. She was just there like a relic from some bygone age. When I was little I was deathly afraid of her but by age seven I had outgrown my fear. It was now her turn to be afraid. When she saw me she gave a little shriek and held her bony

113

chest with claw-like fingers. I hadn't yet reached the self con-
scious age of looking in the mirror before going out so I
didn't know what a sight I presented – tear-streaked face,
bruises on my skin and dishevelled hair. She gasped and
croaked in her scratchy voice:

"What happened to you, girl?"

I hadn't cried since the attack but now my lips trembled at
the memory. "My mother did it," I blurted out and the tears
came down again. Miss Jessie wanted to know if I had been a
bad girl and I said no. "I am always good," I told her and
then she asked:

"Why did she do it then?"

"I asked about my father and she got angry. She always
gets angry when I ask about him."

"That scumbag," Miss Jessie barked out harshly, "I coulda
told her he was no good the first day I laid eyes on him."

"My daddy was a bad man?" I asked, shocked.

"The worst. Ran off with her own sister. Your Ma hasn't
been the same since."

"You mean my daddy isn't dead?"

"Heck no!" said Miss Jessie and I wondered if she realised
she was talking to a child.

"He lives with your aunty two towns over."

I looked at her with my mouth open, my young mind in a
whirl. "You mean I have an aunty and my daddy is still alive?
Wow." Before I could digest this information however my
mother appeared on the landing, hugged tightly in her own
embrace, the wild look still on her face.

Miss Jessie looked at her and said: "This looks bad. Run to
Mrs Green's apartment on the ground floor, dearie, and tell
her to call an ambulance while I keep an eye on your ma."

I'd hardly made two steps when my mother started to descend the stairs.

"Run child," urged Miss Jessie and she gave me a little shove to help me on my way. I took off like I had wings round the corner to Mrs Green's apartment. When I got there I blurted out my request between gulps for air and ran back to the hall. I didn't want to miss anything. When I got back Miss Jessie was stroking my mother's hair. It was a clumsy-looking gesture as if she had never done anything like it before. Relief shone on her face when she saw me, I could tell that she wasn't comfortable being alone with my mother.

"She hasn't said a word, poor thing. I knew this day would come, believe me. He never sends a penny for your upkeep. That's why she has to do what she does to pay the bills."

"What do you mean Miss Jessie?" I asked innocently.

She looked at me crossly for a second as if I should know all there was to know or maybe she was contemplating whether I was old enough to be told. "Why do you think she goes out most nights after working in that infernal factory all day? Because she likes to? Or because she likes leaving you alone? No dearie, she has to or you'd both starve."

It wasn't until many years later that I understood what she meant and it made me cry.

The ambulance arrived fifteen minutes after the call was made. They asked me to repeat what had occurred before they took my mother away, and that's the last I ever saw of her. She went calmly, didn't put up a fight, didn't give me a hug or a kiss, nothing. She didn't even look back as they drove away.

Had I known she was never coming back I might have kicked up a fuss but how was I to know? How is anyone to know these things? In my child's mind I felt free. I was already planning to make something special for dinner which is something I'd been doing since I was seven or eight. I felt like an omelette that night but much to my surprise shortly after the ambulance pulled out a police car drove up. Miss Jessie and I were still standing in front of our building. The two officers, a man and a woman, got out and walked toward us, one of them opened a notebook and said:

"We've been sent to pick up Lina Smiley."

"There's no need. I can look after her till her mother gets back from the hospital," said Miss Jessie.

"And you are?" asked the female officer.

"Just call me Jessie. I'm their landlady."

The officer gave her a dubious look and said: "I admire your offer to help, Jessie, but where Mrs. Smiley is going she won't be back in a hurry."

As if she hadn't already guessed, Miss Jessie asked: "And where is that?"

"She is being sent for psychiatric evaluation. That might take weeks, even months. The law requires that the child be placed in a home if there are no responsible relatives to look after her."

"I see. In that case, she has a father you know. I don't know that he's responsible though but he's family. Flesh and blood is always better than being among strangers."

"I agree but we still have to take her," said the officer and asked for my father's address which, of course, Miss Jessie knew.

I stood by quietly while all of this took place and all I could think of was the omelette I wasn't going to have for dinner after all.

One of them finally spoke to me directly and said: "So you're the little tyke. You look a fright. How about if we take you to your apartment, eh? Fix you up pretty and collect some of your things. What do you say?"

"Alright," I agreed and went into the building. I showered and changed then I took my best clothes which wasn't much and my favourite doll and stuffed it into a shopping bag.

I bade Miss Jessie goodbye with a brave face but I was in turmoil, not knowing what to expect.

The home wasn't bad and I stayed there for about a week before my father came and got me. I didn't recognise him. My mother didn't have pictures and my memory of him had faded. I had gotten a beating once when I asked mom why there weren't any pictures of my father. He seemed happy to have me in his life but I could tell that my aunt was not. They had no children together and while she did not ill-treat me she didn't go out of her way to be kind to me either.

At first I was happy but as the years went by I became disillusioned. Especially when I learned that my mother was never coming home again. I was never taken to see her and when I remembered that Jessie had told me that my father and my aunt were the cause of my mother's mental state I started to resent him and over time that resentment led to outright hatred. It got so bad that I couldn't bear to look at him or my aunt anymore. As soon as I graduated high school I left.

I went back to my old neighbourhood and was surprised to find that Miss Jessie was still alive and still doing what she does best, minding other people's business. She looked twice as old as I remembered; if that was possible. She is using a walker to get around now and I could tell that she is on her last legs but her mind is as sharp as ever. She offered to let me crash with her until I got a job and a place of my own. I accepted gladly. She also gave me the name of the asylum where my mother was interred and I couldn't wait until I turned eighteen when I would be legally allowed to visit her on my own.

Whoever said that you don't really know a person until you live with them knows what they were talking about. Since she spent so much time in the hall I had always imagined Miss Jessie's apartment on the ground floor to be dirty and cluttered. I mean, where would she find the time to clean? I also imagined that a person her age would probably have a lot of mementos as well. How wrong I was! I got the feeling I was walking into a hospital, the spotless rooms were sparsely furnished with just the barest of necessities. No ornaments or decorations of any kind and if she had photographs they were locked away somewhere. Her bedroom was the only room that showed signs of habitation. The single bed was well made but I could see bedroom slippers sticking out beneath the wrinkle-free sheets that covered it. The only other piece of furniture was a nightstand with a reading lamp. On the shade of the lamp hung a crucifix on a string of beads, a Star of David and an image of Buddha. I guessed those represented her cultural identity or she wasn't taking any chances where God was concerned. The door to her closet was closed and I didn't get a peek in there. The second bed-room was used as a laundry room. There were some boxes piled against one wall. The washer and dryer against another. Some clothes hampers and a utility cupboard hugged the oth-er wall. The middle of the room was bare and she said that if I didn't mind sleeping in here she would buy me a small bed or I could sleep on the couch in the living room. The choice was mine.

"Those," she said, pointing to the boxes, "contain some of your Ma's pretty things. I didn't like throwing them away. I left the apartment intact for two years but by then I figured she wasn't coming back so I wrote to your father asking him to bring you along to select what you wanted but the bastard never replied. Sorry dear but some things need to be said. I always reckoned that you'd return some day."

"Thanks a lot. I really appreciate that Miss Jessie."

"Don't mention it. I remember how you used to dress up in her clothes when she went out and come model for me. You remember that?"

"Of course. You remember the red mini dress?" I asked.

"How can I forget? You tripped on the hem and tumbled down the stairs." We both laughed at the memory until tears appeared in our eyes. It was the first time that I can recall ever seeing Miss Jessie laugh. She wiped her eyes and said: "Aye. I laugh now but you gave me such a fright that night. It's a miracle you didn't break a bone or two."

"Yeah. I was lucky."

"Well dearie, the closet in here is free, you can use that. Where are your things?"

"I left them at the bus station."

"Go get them then. What are you waiting for? Christmas?" she almost screeched and hauled herself on her walker back to her accustomed perch.

It took a week of job hunting before I got something that suited me or I should say I was suited for. That week I offered to clean the apartment in return for her generosity but Miss Jessie informed me that she had a cleaning lady who also

119

did laundry that came in twice per week for the past three years. That explained the spotlessness, obviously.

We got to talking one day, Miss Jessie and I, and I asked a question that had been on my mind for as long as I knew her:

"Do you have relatives of any kind?"

"You've got spunk girl. No one has ever dared ask me that before." She grew wistful for a while before she said, "I had a sister once. She migrated to some faraway place and I never heard of her again."

"Have you ever been in love?"

"Bah. What's that? A recipe to give you heartache? No thanks, but I did marry a man that was fool enough to ask me."

"How did that turn out?"

"He died and left me this building."

She said that without emotion or explanation and I left it at that. I figured if she wanted me to know the details she'd fill me in on her own steam. I had one more question though.

"Who'll inherit the building after you?" I asked delicately.

She turned and looked me squarely in the eyes. If she had refused to answer I wouldn't have blamed her. She mulled it over before answering, "You haven't changed, have you? I sold it a couple years back. My money goes to charity when I kick the bucket. Satisfied now girlie?" she croaked, not un-kindly and I smiled shamefacedly and said:

"I guess."

Soon after that conversation I started working and we never had time to say much more than hello to each other but two weeks before my eighteenth birthday Miss Jessie stopped me in the hall as I came in from work. She didn't beat around the bush but told me flat out:

"Your Ma passed away suddenly this morning, dearie. I'm sorry."

I was devastated. And nine years of pent up tears came gushing out when I heard the news.

When we were Alone

Our parents stopped having conversations in colour and the moment it happened we all knew. All they were left with was a mono-chromatic existence that consisted of mostly monosyllabic responses that we had come to learn by heart.

"T"ings ain't getting betta at all."

"Na!"

They knew now how to speak with lips pressed tightly to-gether and faces held stiff in fatigued paralysis.

And this was when we came to love the dark. It provided for us our brightest sparks of colour. We plunged in at the first sight of the shadows hovering welcomingly on the edges of their already dark world. Suddenly we had a time all to ourselves away from their struggles and dying conversations to meet and to escape the overbearing, oppressive sadness of our homes. Gathering in our accustomed spots, our nightlife began. We could once more run with wild abandon while the parents rustled around in the dark trying to find candles and then later flambeaus. For them the darkness was another blight to be faced down; we willingly allowed the darkness to envelop us.

The trees that we raided mercilessly for every last bit of their fruit during the glaring light of day would become our co-conspirators in the dark. Sitting with our backs leaned against their strong trunks, some bleeding from the on-slaughts that we had made on them during the day, we felt their forgiveness and understanding of our desperation. They welcomed our warm backs against their trunks and our noisy chatter under their branches and willingly provided for us what we eagerly sought on those dark nights – a place of es-cape; a place of light and colour.

There were some of us – the more daring ones – who would climb high up to the tallest branches and pretend that they were the ones in charge – the government (it had be-come another one of our catch phrases borrowed from the adult conversations) and they would make loud and crazy proclamations, "I, King of Tree Top Kingdom, hereby de-clare that as of this moment all children in this kingdom are allowed to drink as much milk and eat as many snacks as they please and will hereafter eat breadfruit only once per week if they so please." And we would look up and try to find our pretend king between the darkness of the branches and we would all shout in the general direction of his voice, "All hail our King of Tree Top Kingdom!" And in unison and with voices muffled so as not to alert the adults as to our where-abouts, we would add with snorts and giggles, "So says of our king of Tree Top Kingdom and so shall it be, O good and kind King!" And then the laughter would follow, loud and raucous, and some of us would roll around under those trees convulsing with laughter with tears streaming down our faces.

They – the adults – pretended not to hear us and we were never sure we really wanted to be ignored.

There were stories too. The stories we told were not for the faint of heart and each night our imaginations exploded in a riot of colour right there in the midst of their shadows. We were beckoned by the flames of the flambeaus that danced in the shadows of the houses where we had left the parents. Sometimes when we looked up and through the open windows we could see them inside the houses and we saw their shapes made grotesque by the dim light of the flambeaus. These shadows tickled our imaginations with their smoky figures drawing intriguing patterns on the walls of our homes and on our minds. These were the shadows that sometimes played starring roles in our childishly gruesome tales of 'jumbies' and 'old higues.' Or sometimes they were dragons spitting fire because they had lost their powers and were condemned to a dark and gloomy cave.

Then there were the stories of the tricksters, *Nancy* and *Sensibill and Stupidtybill*. Stories that we were told in the better days when the parents found the time to sit with us on the doorsteps on nights when the hot and stuffy weather forced them outside to catch a breath of 'fresh air'. When we ran out of the stories they had told us about these tricksters we made our own stories with new tricksters and new tricks.

We felt triumphant because we had made the dark our ally and we had it all to ourselves and our imaginations. Our voices pierced the darkness night after night becoming bolder and louder as we chased each other down in seemingly never-ending games of 'Sal pass' and 'Post to post' and 'Jumbie left de piper' and 'Bun down house' and 'One, two, three, red light.' We played those games with fervour on those 'blackout nights' when we still could not understand the reasons for the nightly darkness.

Refusing to lose our colour, we fought obscurity on those nights with our wild stories and our loud games. We never allowed ourselves to be gobbled up by the monster that threatened us. We knew that if we did we would become like them – the parents. We knew that we would become the shadows that they had become without even knowing it.

Then one night we invented our game for the adults. A game that we lured them into and forced them to play with us. It was the 'blackouts' and the ensuing nightly darkness that gave us the power to do that too. It was called "Snake". The moment the lights went out (and we were guaranteed a dark night every night) we would run to our spot.

It was the same spot each night but we chose our victims carefully. They did not know us as well as we knew them. It was always this way with our adults and their preoccupation with 'life' but we knew them well enough. We knew who lived where and with whom and we knew who was just visiting and how often they would visit; we knew the ones who were more distracted than the others and who paid very little attention to the outside world. The quick steppers who were always hustling and bustling tightly wound in their world made complicated by the darkness. Then there were the market ladies who provided our most enjoyable episodes and, of course, there were others who we chose to give a break or pull into our dark world. We knew them all. Choosing a mark for each night became way too easy.

Our lookouts were placed strategically, way out at the head of the street and as soon as a suitable mark approached they would send the warning hoot:

"Coo, coo, coo, coo."

This was our signal to get prepared for the action. The Snake was prepared way in advance. During the day the boys would get it ready. An old bicycle tube was ideal, for it would give us an almost life-like undulation when we dragged it slowly through the bushes. It became even more life-like after the boys had made it more elastic by beating it against the trunk of a tree. To this now nicely wiggly rubber, we added a long piece of dependable string, one that would run the width of the road and would give us enough leverage when we hid behind our tree. We could never figure out how that one tree could conceal so many of us but the darkness helped.

When we heard the hoot we would be ready. And as the mark made its way toward us we were never nervous. Anyone of us would be able to pull the Snake for we all had a steady hand, but we took turns allowing each of us a chance at the fun. As the marks came closer, we read their movements and we responded. We waited patiently, with the confidence of time forever being on our side, until they were close enough to sense the movements yet far enough to give us enough time for repeated warning pulls. Timing was everything and we had all learnt that. The first jerk of the string was quick and sharp, a short snap of the wrist that sent a perceptible shiver through the bushes. It was intended to alert the mark. The bushes would respond with its customary rustle. And the mark would respond with its predicted pause. A quick stop and an upright jerking of the body as the head snapped to attention and the eyes darted forward and commenced its useless and feeble penetration of the darkness in the direction which the movement was sensed. It was the moment of our first stifled laughter. The moment when the adult – it was always an adult, never any children for we knew that we could not fool any children; well, maybe except the really young ones and they were never allowed to roam the streets on these 'blackout' nights – would pause, frozen in a comical pose (sometimes one forgotten foot hanging loosely in mid-air and arms dangling aimlessly) as they searched the darkness for the unknown. We could see their outlines clearly in the dark because the moon was our friend, never theirs.

The fun started then. These adults, who during the daylight hours were so self-assured, so in control you would never doubt anything they said, would be something else to behold on those 'blackout' nights in the middle of a familiar street lit only by the light of the moon and facing some unforeseen danger in the bushes. So we watched them and made them dance to our rubber Snake. After that first jerk we had them; every time. Their steps were checked. Their movements belonged to us and we pulled the strings. We gave them enough time after that first pull to compose themselves, allowing them time to be convinced that it was their imagination. We would sense it when they were comfortable again and could smell them reasserting themselves against the intrusion of the dark. After all, this was their neighbourhood and there was nothing for them to be afraid of. They lived here and were the ones in charge. And they would take off again; this time more purposefully, more determinedly, more bravely, with each step pounding louder than ever.

Then the second jerk came. The second jerk had to be more forceful. There had to be sounds drawn from the bushes that would reach the mark way up in his head. This second pull was meant to stop him cold, and because we were experts we always did. We added our accompanying sounds at this second pull. Old rusted cans were found to be the best at producing a horrifyingly grating sound as the Snake moved its way up the sides of the gutters. Another skilful twitch of the wrist would allow the end of the now active Snake to hit the water just right and this sound to travel quickly up through the bushes. The mark always heard that sound, that dreadful, sharp splash. It was that last pull coupled with the sounds and movements that drew the fear out of their bellies and into the darkness. The fear that they emitted from their bodies was what must have transformed a wiggling piece of rubber into a monster of the dark. Our Snake crept closer and closer to them and none of them ever moved right away. It always fascinated us the most to see each of them standing, transfixed eyes plastered on the long, black, moving beast. Why is it they never tried to run away from that Snake? That is what we would do. But the adults never did that. It was as if our Snake was challenging them for their spot in the neighbourhood and they could never let that happen.

And so we held them there on that spot with our rubber Snake advancing and retreating, and them with their determination to destroy this threat in the dark, caught in a dance of fear. The first steps started backward and forward and then sideways in a light sway – testing the Snake's perception. We danced with them, moving the Snake to their predictable movements, never allowing it to remain still. Their head movements came then–sharp turns to the left and right–and we knew they were searching madly blindly for a weapon of any sort in the belly of the dark. All of us, except the one manning the Snake, would roll with quiet laughter as the adult mark rushed around trying to find a weapon suitable enough to destroy this danger. A crazed search ensued everywhere but in the bushes with one eye still on the Snake whose movement had been reduced to slithers just as reassurance of its presence.

Then the final pull – one that required the full strength of our arms as we brought the string up and over our heads so that the Snake would appear to leap out of the bushes high in the air just so that the mark could get a look at its black out-line, and then back down in its hiding place. This was what we were waiting for. The mark would seemingly go crazy. This was the moment of confirmation. It was not the imagi-nation any longer. The threat was real, tantalising and tangi-ble. They would rush to the edge of the bushes, all caution dissipating with the unabashed boldness of the intruder. And the blows would start raining wildly in every direction, each blow accompanied by a string of words that were intended to teach a crucial lesson in obedience.

"Yuh tek me for a joker? I's a big man/woman going 'bout me business and yuh wan run out at me from between bushes. I gon show you who I is. Tek dis and dis and dis and when de looking for yuh in de morning de gon see yuh sprawled out dead pon yuh belly like de snake you is."

At that precise moment, no longer restrained by the arms of the dark, we would scamper away wildly in various direc-tions carried by our laughter ringing loud, clear and childish and leaving behind in the dark the bent body of an adult beat-ing furiously at a piece of old rubber.

The beach awaits

As I sat there waiting for the ambulance, I found myself making peace with my Maker. The phrase "my life flashed in front my eyes" was suddenly reality to me. I started bargaining with God that I'd rather have broken limbs instead of internal injuries. The pain was excruciating and there was no identifying the source, all I knew was that I could not breathe properly and my head hurt, my son was holding my hand all through the ordeal, my husband was somewhere lying on the ground, and my daughter, where was my daughter? Was she alright? No one told me anything, but then if they did, it was all incomprehensible. Why was it taking so long? Has it been minutes or hours since the accident? How did my son reach us so fast? Where did all these people come from? Why was that woman crying? Where is my husband, why isn't he coming to get me out? Am I trapped? Or, am I dying and they think there is no point in saving my life? I wouldn't either, if I would remain a vegetable forever. Where are all the people I love, where are they when I need them? Why did this thing happen to us?

Why did God let this happen? Was this a lesson he was trying to teach me? If so, why involve my family? This is my fault, I knew it, but why not punish me alone? At least my son is not hurt, he was not with us, that I remember! I am sure he would help me, but, why isn't he getting me out?

Oh! How my head hurts; I am hearing all these voices. Why is everyone speaking all at the same time? I cannot focus. I am scared God, please let me be with my family, let them be alright, please don't separate us. Suddenly, I felt myself falling, slowly at first and then faster and faster. Darkness engulfed me and I became more scared. Kirk, Kirk, I kept calling my son, but he did not answer and I felt all alone in the dark, I was always afraid of the dark, and now I was submerged in this abysmal place and very, very scared and very alone—

Mom, mom, my son kept calling me.

I hear you son but I cannot see you. Please pull me out; please help me!

Mom, I am here, can you hear me? Mom you are going to be alright, do you hear me? Mom, I love you, dad loves you, Lily loves you, we are all here waiting for you, please come back, we need you, we cannot live without you!

Oh my darling, I love you all too, but just pull me out and I'll be okay... why is he not hearing me?

Mom remember when Lily and I were little and when we were scared you would hug us and say that everything would be alright? Well mom I need a hug right now, please wake up and give me a hug as I am hugging you, can you feel me hugging you mom? I am right here, I am not leaving you, I would remain here as long as it takes because we love you and that's what families do, they stay for each other, they don't leave.

131

But, where is Lily? Where is dad? How come I cannot hear them? Where are they son?

Mom, he was saying, remember the day I shared my dream with you, remember the day I came home from school and told you that I knew what I wanted to do with my life, that I wanted to become a pilot, and you hugged me and said that if that is what I wanted you would ensure that my dream comes true? Well, ,mom, it is finally happening, and I need you here with me, I must have you by my side when I achieve my dream, it wouldn't mean anything anymore without you by my side, please mom, come back to me… I mean to us… despite the numerous changes around us, you are the one constant in our lives. You are the sole reason for my bare existence, I am sorry if I caused you any grief during my growing up years, mom, I ask you to forgive me and I promise not to cause you anymore hurt.

Son, you never caused me any grief, the day you were born was one of the happiest days of my life, I have enjoyed every minute I spent with you, you have brought me so much joy, I cannot imagine life without you and Lily, oh! My lovely Lily, where is my beautiful little girl? But why am I still here? Why don't you just hold my hand and pull me out son? Where is dad, why doesn't he help me? Why is it taking so long? Son, do you hear me?

Mom, mom, do you hear me?

Yes son! I hear your sweet voice, I can feel your touch, I feel you pulling me, I can see you, I can see your face, I can see you son, oh! You are so beautiful. Why are you crying son? Don't cry, I am here.

Oh! Mom, you are here, you are going to be alright.

Where is Lily and dad, son?

They'll be here soon, the doctor said one visitor at a time.

But, I need to see them. Tell me, how long have I been here?

Mom, you have been in a coma for three months. You, dad and Lily have had a car accident, a drunk driver hit you. Kirk was talking very slowly, pain etched on his face with tears streaming from his eyes, and I was very scared. Mom, he said, dad and Lily died that day and you went into a coma. I am sorry mom. He started to sob uncontrollably. I was in awe, I couldn't grasp what he was saying, but now I understood why I wasn't hearing their voices while I was comatose. I felt myself consoling him, instead of being consoled. How are we going to go on? How are we going to pick up the pieces of our shattered lives? How will we survive this? How can I live without my husband and my little girl? Why were their lives snatched away from me? Why did God take away my daughter? I want my family back, I want my family whole again. Why didn't I die too? Isn't God supposed to be a *loving* God?

Mom, said my son, breaking my reverie, dad is with Lily and he will take care of her until we meet again. God is not cruel, he left you with me, and dad with Lily. Isn't that what you taught us, that we have to take care of each other? I took my son's face into my hands and wiped his tears. Yes my son! God is not cruel, he is good and wise, he has been good to us. At that moment I prayed to Him to take care of them until we met again, notwithstanding the fact that I said it with a heavy heart.

Released from the hospital, my son and I began to piece together the remaining bits of our lives. To say it was difficult is an understatement, it was extremely hard, impossible even, to go on. Returning to our house was challenging; I said house because it was not a home to me anymore; a home is supposed to be a happy place with a family, a home is where the heart is, and my family was not whole anymore and my heart was ripped out of my chest. There was a void, a hole and a dull ache where my heart used to be. I was very remorseful and resentful all the time. I know I was not being fair to my son and I had to be there for him, but I was so depressed I did not know how to be normal again.

Going into my daughter's room was very heart-wrenching, the many pictures on the wall, the trophies she had won for academic achievements, the many hopes and dreams she had, the bright future that awaited her, all snatched away in a minute. I take comfort in believing that she did not suffer too much, that it was painless as possible. Teddy bears lay strewn across the room. Everything would be left as is. I lay on her bed. Her scent from her pillow filled my nostrils and overtook my entire being. Tears welled up in my eyes and I cried and cried until I fell asleep. When I awoke it was dark outside. Good. Probably that was the way to go through the day; sleep day and night. The day was okay but at nights it proved very difficult.

Mom, are you there? Why is the house dark? Mom, are you okay?

Yes, son, I am fine. He came and found me in Lily's room.

Oh, mom don't do this, and he sat on the floor and said, Lily was really messy wasn't she? I remember you always yelling at her to clean up her room.

Despite the pain I smiled. Yes, I remember. Oh but how I treasured the mess now, because this was how I wanted to remember her, the way she was, and I made a little promise to

God that if he brought her back I would not care about a clean room again, I would not yell at her ever again. Silly isn't it? A grown woman saying this to God, but I guess one in pain would say anything.

Mom, Kirk broke the silence, I brought dinner. Come let's eat.

My son is being so brave, assuming the role of head of the family, he pretending to be so normal all the while he is hurting. I am the one who is supposed to be taking care of him, and he is being the grown up one here.

Food to me was not important. What was important was getting things back to normal. The nights were lonely and sad, I missed my husband, my friend, we built a family and life together, and he had left Kirk and I behind. At times I got angry at him: how can he be so selfish; how can he just go and leave us; didn't the vows "forever" mean anything? He was a good husband and the best father ever, I felt comfort in knowing that wherever he was, Lily was with him, and they would console each other and there was no more pain and suffering where they were. To be honest I would have preferred to be there with them, but I believe that I was saved for a reason and that reason was to be there for my son, because he had to achieve great things in his life and he needed my help.

Kirk was now a pilot, he finally realised his dream, his father and sister would have been so proud of him as was I.

Mom, are you ready? It was Kirk's graduation.

Yes son, I'm ready.

Before closing the door I glanced backward, and my eyes fell on a family photo, and my heart sank. Today's photo would contain only two people. Of course Kirk was valedictorian. In his speech he spoke of family and the importance of it, his eyes never leaving mine the whole time, his family was so proud of him, and I know his father and sister were looking down at him from Heaven. Kirk was offered a job overseas right after graduation, but he turned it down, his reason was that it was too soon. He said he couldn't leave just yet, it would be too much for me, I told him to go, I'll be alright, but he insisted that he work right here, until I was better, but would I ever be better?

I could not go back to work, I could not face the world, I could not go back to being normal, I felt guilty for leaving them behind, they could not go forward and I did not want to either. I just could not go on like everything was alright. I was broken and nothing could fix me up. My son could not bear his mother sinking into this depressive state. He made sure he was there as much as he could be but he realised I was not getting better. One day he came home early and said:

Mom, come on, get dressed, let's go.

Where? I asked. I don't feel like going out.

Mom, I think this will be good for you, come on, get dressed, let's go. Trust me mom.

That I did, I did love and trust him, so I gave in.

After travelling for awhile, Kirk stopped in front a moderate-looking house.

Who lives here? I asked him.

Come out and you will see, he said.

We went to meet the people who lived there, there was a man whose arm was in a cast, a woman and a little girl, they appeared to be a middleclass family. They asked us to sit. Obviously my son had met them before.

Mom, this is Mr. Charles, his wife Carol and their daughter Stacey. Mom, Mr. Charles was the driver who hit dad's car that day.

I felt all the blood drain from my body. My legs went numb–good thing I was sitting. My eyes searched my son's: how could you do this? How could you bring me to meet the person who killed my family?

Mr. Charles spoke: Ma'am, I am very sorry, I can't say how sorry I am for what I caused. My wife and I live in remorse every day. I regret that day, I wish I could just take it all back.

With all the resolve in me, I asked him, What happened to your arm?

It broke in three places, he said, the doctors say that I may never regain full use of it again.

Good! my mind screamed. I took a deep breath and said nothing aloud. No one spoke for a little while. How old is your daughter? I asked him.

Twelve, he said, she is in school.

Was she in the vehicle with you and your wife?

No! he said, she did not want to go.

Lily, that's my daughter, she did not want to go to the beach, that's where we were going, but I wanted to go, maybe I should have left her home too.

No one said anything at that point. The silence was deafening.

Their faces were so sad, and then I realised: *they are really remorseful*. So, I mustered the courage to ask him:

Is it true what they say; that you were drunk the day–

I couldn't say anymore.

Yes! he said, almost in a whisper and then, I am sorry, in an even softer tone and bent his head.

I looked around I saw tears in his wife's eyes.

After what seemed like hours, I said: Well, I hope your arm heals and I do hope you regain full use of it, I really do.

I am not sure he believed me. I am not sure I even believed myself but I knew what I felt, and I cannot explain it, but I really meant it.

I looked at my son, and he was staring at me with bewildered eyes. I motioned to him that it was time to leave.

We left with a simple goodbye, no handshakes, no hugs, no we'll keep in touch.

Back in the car, my son asked, Mom, are you okay?

I turned to him with a smile and said thanks!

He patted my hand and said, We are going to be okay mom.

I breathed a sigh of relief and thought to myself: yes, we are going to be okay. I think what my son brought me today was the greatest gift I ever got, he brought me closure. Not closure to all the pain, that would take years, but closure to the hate and animosity I felt since that fateful day, closure in knowing what happened. I looked through the window and stared towards Heaven and pictured my loved ones smiling back at me.

Yes, we'll be alright.

Dis anime ting again

The sound of clashing metal echoed piercingly throughout the tranquil night skies, shrouding the atmosphere in a cloak of suspense. Blemished fingers stained with blood trembled feverishly as the lone girl stood her ground against the hell that was soon to befall her. Who would have thought that an innocent excursion across the border to deliver medical supplies to the neighbouring village would have turned into a night beleaguered with murder and the shrill cries of wounded victims as they were brought to their untimely demise?

Never had she expected her life to change so drastically. The girl mentally mourned for the loss of her loved ones whose bodies now lay lifeless at her feet, their facial expressions permanently frozen with death. She was the only one left standing now and she cringed as she stared fearfully into the cold eyes of the *monsters* that stood before her.

All ten beasts of death stood surrounding her weakened form, circling her hungrily like wolves before their prey. Even though they had already taken down most of her clan, it was still not enough to satisfy their lust for blood. They could not leave her alone. They would have rather watched her fall than lose the chance to listen to her scream and beg for mercy at the feeling of their blades piercing her premature flesh.

Though she stood her ground against them. Though she shakily yet courageously clutched the long sword that was once forged by her presently deceased father and was her last hope of defending herself against the impending onslaught... it was still not enough to save her. It was inevitable that these ten beasts not only outnumbered her but also outranked her as a swordsman. Compared to these men whose own swords were scarred and stained with years of experience, she was an amateur. Even though, she had desperately attempted to survive up to this point. To them, her faith had already been sealed. She was *dead*.

Cautiously, the men drew their swords and began to advance towards the girl. Her heart stopped beating as the fear rose rapidly in her chest. This was it. She was finished. Without warning, the men attacked. From all sides they came, the cold fangs of their blades extended to penetrate her. In that moment, the girl's legs gave in to their exhaustion, allowing her body to fall in defeat and succumb to the oblivion that was to engulf her soul.

"Insolent fools. How dare you raise your sword to a young child? How dare you stain your blades with the blood of the innocent?

You don't even deserve to call yourselves samurais.

Now you shall die by my sword, unworthy children of men–"

In the blink of an eye and by the flash of a sword, all time stood still. Not a sound penetrated this deadened silence. Not even the shrill cries of the ten bandits were heard amongst the stillness as they were dealt their unfortunate punishment and delivered to their creator.

Slowly, the young girl lifted her head and opened her eyes from the bed of grass she had fallen onto during her collapse and what she saw before her almost stopped her heart from beating.

What was previously an army of cruel-hearted mountain bandits was now reduced to a dismantled heap of flesh and blood for now... all ten men were *dead*. Their heads had been sliced clean off of their bodies.

The young child gawped at this blood-stained mess that was the remnants of her previous assaulters, too astonished to even breathe and she wondered to herself: who could have done such a thing. Though she was thankful to be ridden of those horrible men, even she did not think that they deserved a death so torturous.

Who? Who did this? It was then she saw *him*.

From within the darkness of the night, he came. A towering male figure shrouded in a flowing cloak as dark as the night itself, the ends of the cloak tarnished and jagged from past battles. His face and body were kept completely concealed, the only part of him visible being his eyes. Eyes that were amber with youth yet gray with maturity and the knowledge of experience. It was these same eyes that glared sharply at the defenceless infant at his feet, leaving her transfixed under his gaze like a sheep caught before the butcher. In the man's withered hands he wielded a long sword—a *katana* to be more specific.

Its hilt was as white as the snow that came in the winter, an eerie colour which contrasted dissonantly with the man's attire. But its blade was what captured the child's attention. Its blade was forged of pure silver, its shimmering surface emulated by the light of the lone moon hovering above.

However it was not *that* that the child was looking at. It was the *blood*. The blood that stained the curved edge of the blade. The girl gasped at the realisation that this man had killed those bandits. He *alone* murdered an army of ten men with one strike of his sword.

A masterful skill that deemed him dangerous in the eyes of the young girl. Immediately, the girl's hand gripped the hilt of her father's sword.

He won't be able to kill her if she struck first; at least those were the child's thoughts. Unfortunately for her, the man had already anticipated her move.

"It takes a brave man to raise his sword to a swordsman of my calibre," the man spoke, "all the same; I do not plan to die today. You on the other hand child, shall I put you out of your misery too?"

In the same swiftness that allowed him to easily slaughter the bandits, the man rendered the girl helpless as he knocked her weapon from her hands without difficulty. The child herself had not seen him coming and now she sat against the grass, staring wide-eyed at the blade of the man's sword as he held it threateningly to her throat.

"Well? Do you?" the man repeated grimly.

The child only shook her head solemnly. "Do what you wish. It won't do you any good. What do I have to live for now? The bodies of my family lie dead at your feet all because of them," the child hissed harshly through clenched teeth, glaring at the bandits' corpses, "so if you want to kill me then do it. But know that there will also come a time when you will be punished with the same fate."

The girl had expected her remark to provoke the man but to her surprise, he chuckled, as if *impressed* by her audacity. "A bold statement for one so young," he commented. "If that is what you wish then have it your way."

The man raised his sword. The child closed her eyes tightly, mentally preparing herself for the blow. But for the second time she had underestimated the man for he did not strike. Instead he sheathed his sword and now held it out to the child, who appeared bewildered by his actions.

"My sword. Hold it," the man instructed. Obediently, the girl took hold of the sword and balanced it in her hands. "The name of this sword is *White Fang*," the man continued, "one day; you too shall wield a sword just like this one, given the proper training. Do you have a name young one?"

"Tsubaki," the girl replied softly.

"Tsubaki, you possess a heart of both bravery and strength and one with a heart such as yours deserves life over death," the man stated wisely, "but in order to keep living, you must become stronger. I can teach you how to survive."

"Tsubaki, I am *Ryuusuke Hibachi* but from now on, you will address me as your *sensei*," the man declared, "for I will teach you how to wield a sword. I will teach you how to fight with honour and *kill* without mercy."

And it was in that very moment when Tsubaki's life changed forever.

"TAQUEESHA!"

"What?"

Immediately Taqueesha Belmontes awoke from the world within the black and white pages of the comic book she had been reading and returned to the reality of the form five classroom she was presently seated in.

She was met with the disgruntled face of her classmate, Chandelle, who stood hovering over her desk with her arms folded.

"Miss Chandelle Harris, wha' you yelling my name so hard for?" Taqueesha asked arrogantly.

"Gyal, you know how long I calling you but ya so reading ya little book dat ya ain't even hear meh," Chandelle grunted, "speaking of which, what you was so busily reading during Maths? Doh feel I ain't see ya. I bet ya ain't even hear one ting de teacher say."

Taqueesha rolled her eyes at her friend as she continued skimming her eyes through the pages of the book.

"Whaz dat?" Chandelle asked, eyeing the book on Taqueesha's desk curiously as she propped herself against the seat in front of her.

"It's one of dem *manga* books," Taqueesha answered, holding up the book, "y'know de Japanese *anime* ting."

"You and dis anime ting again! Chile like you *obsessed* with dis ting," Chandelle said. "You wasn't just reading one of dat de other day?"

"Yeah but dat was anudder different one. Dat one was de *D.N.Angel* dat I did borrow from Shanice in de nex' class," Taqueesha said, "dis one is *Tsubaki Chronicles*."

"And what dis one about now?" Chandelle asked.

"It about dis gyal name Tsubaki and she supposed to be dis real bad samurai. Daz what dey does call dem people who does fight with de long sword and ting," Taqueesha explained, "anyways right now she tracking down dis man who did kill she master. Basically de whole story is 'bout Tsubaki's development as a samurai as she tries to kinda improve she skills nah and become strong enuff to avenge she master's death. I only just started reading it but it going real good so far," Taqueesha added.

"Ya now start but already ya know de book back and front," Chandelle said, "if only ya was dis interested in ya Maths."

"Ya understand. Gyal sometimes I wish anime was a subject for CXC," Taqueesha commented, "if dat was the case den I wudda pass with flying colours. Dey ain't even have to gimme de exam, just hand me meh scholarship one time and I gone."

Chandelle laughed lightly. "Ya sounding jus like meh brudder," she said, "every night, like clock wuk, is like de boy does want to beat me and mammie for de TV. He always want to watch dis same anime ting dat you like."

"Which anime he does watch?"

"Ya asking me? Gyal from what I see is plenty. I cah even count dem on meh hands. And if he not watching it on de TV, he on de computer watching it on YouTube. Cah even check Facebook fus he on it all de time watching dis same anime ting," Chandelle said, "but right now he real like dis one anime. I cah remember de name but is someting with dis boy. Some Narado... or Nurutoro—"

"You mean... *Naruto?*"

"Me ain't even know. Is some show wit dis chupid-looking, blonde boy running around some village in de bush in buss-eye orange clothes." Chandelle said.

"Dat is Naruto self," Taqueesha said, "but Chandelle, I didn't know you does watch Naruto."

"I don't. I doh even like de show especially dat chupid boy," Chandelle grumbled indifferently.

"What wrong with Naruto?"

"I doh like he. Fus he does geh me vex," Chandelle scoffed, "he haff dis annoying ting he does always say. 'Believe it!' Throughout de whole show, everyting is a 'Believe it; believe it!' Believe what? Chupidie!" she added with a steups.

"But daz de boy catchphrase and everybody know Naruto for dat. Wha wrong with you?" Taqueesha uttered defensively. "Besides not all de time Naruto does say dat. In fact later in de series he stops saying de 'Believe it' ting. But in de Japanese version, he always saying he catchphrase. In de jap, he does say *dattebayo.*"

"Datte-who?"

"Never mind."

"Wait, you does watch it in English *and* Japanese? You ain't easy," Chandelle said, staring at her friend in disbelief.

"Well dem English people who does dub de show taking too damn long to bring out new episodes so I does watch de original jap instead cause dat way ahead," Taqueesha said. "The anime episodes are originally made in Japan, it's just dem Americans does put it in de English for we to understand."

"But how you does understand dem jap people with dey ching-chong language?" Chandelle asked.

"My fren, 'ching-chong' is Chinese. Dere is a difference between Chinese and Japanese," Taqueesha implied smartly, "besides, dere is someting called subtitles. De subtitles are in English so all I does do is just read de ting off de screen and I know what de characters saying."

"Well boy, only you people who real like dis ting haff de patience for dat," Chandelle said. "Me? I will just stick with meh *Family Guy*. Dat does go down good."

"Yeah Family Guy *a'ight*," Taqueesha commented.

"But you like de anime ting better?" Chandelle said.

Taqueesha nodded.

"I doh get it. Why allyuh like dis ting?" Chandelle inquired, "Is de action dat allyuh does like? I does see it in Naruto. Dese little children running through de bush throwing knife and ting at one anudder. Ah set of blood spilling all over de ground like ketchup on KFC. Only violence to pollute de poor children mind. Shame. Shame."

"Oh right and wen Baby Stewie does be saying all dem bad ting like de life of a wife is ended by de knife, dat not corrupting de children mind?" Taqueesha said.

"There is a difference. Baby Stewie is kicks. Naruto is just chupid," Chandelle said frankly.

"Ya never even watch de show properly so how you know it chupid?" Taqueesha said, "Besides anime isn't always bout action and violence. Anime is basically about everything dat ya could tink of. If ya look around dere is an anime for practically *anyting* from dem ones about de sci-fi ting to romance and even comedy. If you is a person who real like dem fantasy ting with de vampires and de werewolves, dere are plenty anime about dat too, like dis one called *Vampire Knight*... and *Blood Plus*. Dem two real good. Dere are even anime about teenagers like we who in high school and haff to deal with de same problems with mad teachers, overprotective parents and bullies and other tings," Taqueesha added.

"So... what makes dis anime ting so special dat people hook on it?" Chandelle asked. "I know one of de reasons will haff to be the art 'cause if dere is one ting I could say bout anime is dat de art does look real nice. Dem jap people real talented to come up with dat."

"Dat true but it's not just de art dat draws people in," Taqueesha said. "I dunno. It's not something dat I could exactly explain. I dunno what really makes anime special. Other fans would haff dere own opinions of why dey like it. I just know dat de reason I like it is because it's different and dat is what gets me to read and watch it. Anime is different than anyting dat I haff seen in my life. I does watch a lot of cartoons and none of dem can come to compare to anime. It is just too good. Look, in order for you to really understand and appreciate anime, you will haff to experience it for yaself, dats all I could say," Taqueesha suggested. "Watch de anime and ya might like it. If not, den ya missing out."

Chandelle touched her index finger to her chin in thought and considered what her classmate had just told her. "I tink I might take ya word on dat cause really and truly de ting not so bad. I just do haff de patience to actually sit down and watch de ting like you. Ya know how I am already," Chandelle said, smirking to herself. "Who knows, maybe one of dese nights I will join Barry and watch some Naruto. I haff no choice but to do dat until it done."

"Well ya haff a *long* wait cause Naruto is over four hundred episodes and it still ain't done," Taqueesha said.

Chandelle nearly fell off her seat. "FOUR HUN-DRED! Oh jeez-an-ages!"

"Yeah, so ya better get a head start and let Barry fill you in on wat going on so far," Taqueesha said. "Who knows, maybe de same chupid boy who ya didn't like before might just end up being ya favourite character in de whole show."

Chandelle made a sound which Taqueesha could only describe as a cross between a cough and a high-pitched laugh. "Ah will see," was what she said.

Just then, the bell rang, bringing the brief recess period to an end. One by one, the students of the form five class piled out of their homeroom with their books in their hands on their way to their respective classes.

"What class we haff now?" Taqueesha asked as she finally closed the manga comic, securing it between one of her text books.

Chandelle checked her timetable. "Bio. Lovely," she said dryly, "I hope he not here. I really cah take no lecture bout photosynthesis dis and osmosis dat. I ain't able. I feel I will sleep in he class."

"Ah yes, sleeping in class is definitely a quality of an ideal St. Francois Student," Taqueesha commented sarcastically.

"Thank you," Chandelle answered with a wry smile, "and what bout you missy? Doh lemme ketch ya reading dat same anime book in de man class, ya hear meh? Put it away!"

Taqueesha merely rolled her eyes at her friend's comment. "Ah will see."

Troubles bourne

At six weeks the dreams started. I tried to blame it on my conscience but a stronger more irrational part of me made me believe that it was some sort of communication from my unborn child...from my never-to-be-born, unborn child. In the dream I was at a relative's house, sitting on the verandah, shade being cast from the shadow of a tall coconut tree. There was a baby in my arms, a girl... I could only guess that it was her. I was certain it was her. She was beautiful and she looked like me. I stared at her in awe, wondering to myself if it could be possible for me to manufacture such beauty. Then, without time seeming to have forwarded, her lips closed around my nipple and she sucked. I felt the tug of her lips on my breast as though it was a real thing, flinching as I was jolted from my sleep.

That was the first dream, the others that followed all held to the same pattern, a beautiful baby, always a girl, tugging at my heartstrings, trying ineffectively to weaken my resolve. It was all a useless attempt on her part. My mind was already made up and I would not go back on my decision. She would die and I would be the one to kill her. I would kill her because I was selfish, because I still resided in that state where my needs were the most important, where my wants trumped all else. I was twenty two years old with few friends I could claim and even less familial connections. The word mother was as foreign to me as a cold winter day; I had not had one to love or to emulate. Yet here was the world demanding it of me.

One mistake, they always say that one mistake is all it took but I'd never imagined that my life could turn out to be such a cliché. Not me... not someone as intelligent, as worldly as I. What a laugh. I may have been knowledgeable but I certainly wasn't responsible. Responsible adults didn't have unprotected sex then commit murder. I shuddered at the thought. Hands stained with blood in a red so permanent it would never be cleaned.

The actual conception is not as important to me as the reason behind it. I did not have the excuse of being in love nor could I blame my youth or my upbringing. The act meant nothing to me. It meant less than nothing. I can't even summon details to describe my passion. It was nothing more than me taking advantage of the use of another human being's body for sexual release. I had used the sexual release as a sort of emotional release for I had been running away from a pileup of problems. I knew within a matter of two weeks that I was pregnant. I knew it definitely and so I hesitated to purchase a home test as I knew it would only confirm my fears. Still, on a swelteringly hot day I found myself walking towards a pharmacy on the southern main road in Enterprise, Chaguanas, to purchase a pregnancy test. As I waited in line to make my request I felt as though life was using the opportunity to mock me and to laugh at my fears for it seemed that only baby items were on display, surrounding me, closing in on me, my personal house of horrors. The wait seemed to last hours as I made my way to the front counter and the waiting salesgirl. My body trembled even with the constant fever that I had been burdened with for the past week. I made my request, using proper diction in an effort to ensure that I would not have to repeat my query. She looked at me, a girl of about eighteen, and I could feel her sympathy as she took in my miserable expression. Typically, I would resent her obvious pity but I was so depressed myself that it was welcomed. I walked the five minutes to my office, mumbling to my boss that I had returned before locking myself in the bathroom. I speed-read through the instructions that were aped to the small plastic packet before following them, making sure not to make any kind of error. Then I set aside the test and began my five-minute wait. A chant repeated itself in my head:

"Two lines mean pregnant, one and everything's okay; two lines mean pregnant, one and everything's okay."

Not even a full two minutes had passed before I peeked in time to see the formation of the second line developing. I cursed and quickly grabbed the apparatus and flung it into the bin. I washed my hands and exited the bathroom going back to work consoling myself with inane thoughts.

"*The test was faulty,*" I told myself.

"*What did I expect after buying it in Chaguanas?*" I thought disgustedly.

I was raised in the highly developed west and so considered anything outside of the Port of Spain area to be backward and inferior. The fact that the pregnancy test was faulty

152

proved only to validate my point. I waited a full week before getting another test and when I did I made certain to have my best friend with me as I needed some type of moral support. I repeated my actions from the first test with meticulous care, and waited the full five minutes as prescribed. I asked my friend to check the results for me.

"What's it supposed to say?" she asked.

"Two means pregnant, one means not." I was biting my nails.

She walked towards the counter and looked down at the test.

"Well... I definitely see two lines."

I stared at her, my eyes reflecting my horror at her response. I walked quickly to the test and let my eyes see what she had already verbally confirmed. I walked out of my empty kitchen in my brand new empty apartment and walked toward the bathroom. Then I walked back to the kitchen. I walked again towards the bathroom. I dropped to the floor, giving freedom to a painful, wretched cry. I tried using my hands to hold myself together but it was no use. I was falling apart. My world was over; my life would never be my own. The word abortion never crossed my mind. I just kept seeing myself burdened with this baby, a clearly unwanted addition. There was no doubt that I would come to terms with it and learn to love it but at that moment it was the enemy. The alien being intent on taking over my dismal life. I felt arms encircle me and my best friend was there whispering soothing words. Empty words. Making promises she would never keep. I called the fetus's father, the person who had freely given his sperm to create the creature inside of me. I informed him that he would soon be a daddy for the second time. His reaction was the opposite of my own; he was calm and careful with his words. I wanted to die. If I was dead I wouldn't have to deal with this.

For the next three weeks I accepted that I would be joining the world of single parents. I accepted the fact that I would be nothing more than a statistic. It infuriated me but I was resigned to my fate. I was resigned to the fact that there would be no more shopping expeditions or girls' night out, no more treating myself to the occasional dinner at a trendy restaurant or buying five-hundred-dollar dresses. My money and my time would all go to her. I belonged to her in a way that she didn't belong to me. I had begun thinking of her as a girl and had assigned a name to her in my mind. I called her Love and when my friends complained that I would give her a complex I ignored them because she was my Love, and I would love her and take care of her in a way my mother never loved or took care of me. It all seemed as though things would work out.

Then the problems I was running from started catching up to me along with some brand new ones. My ex-boyfriend, the love of my life, started emotionally blackmailing me, telling me over and over again that I was unfit to be a parent and that I was careless and irresponsible. Things that I already knew but hurdles I felt I could conquer until they were tossed carelessly in my face. My manager at my job let me know that because business was slowing down I would have to be let go. They could no longer afford the luxury of an administrative assistant. I felt hopeless. I was pregnant, would soon be unemployed, my rent was due in a couple of weeks and things were looking awful. I started feeling sick almost immediately, vomiting after every meal, it came to the point that I could only consume soup. I started getting stomach pains and my temperature was always higher than normal. I had no money; well at least I didn't have enough for a doctor's appointment. I tried going to the public hospitals. I tried both Port of Spain and Mt. Hope but was informed that unless I had complications and a doctor referred me to them, they wouldn't be able to help me. Mt. Hope referred me to a health center, though, and so with diminished hope, I took a maxi-taxi on the priority bus route and headed to Macoya. After getting directions from a passerby, I walked into a narrow street and the health center came into view. Some men were relaxing under a tree outside of the premises and started calling out to me in an effort to get my attention. I wanted to scream at them to leave me alone. *Couldn't they tell that I was pregnant?*

The health center was empty of patients. The only person immediately visible to me was the security officer. I asked her for the doctor and she pointed behind me. When I turned around I saw two women sitting behind a counter, a glass partition separating them from me. I walked toward them, taking deep breaths as I could feel my anxiety building. I told them that I believed I was pregnant and that I was seeking confirmation and also some sort of aid as I did not know what my next step was. The first female to speak had a stethoscope placed around her neck; I assumed she was the doctor.

"What do you mean you want to confirm if you're pregnant? Did you take a pregnancy test?" she asked.

"Yes I did and it said positive."

"Well then you're pregnant," she said rudely.

The girl whom she had been speaking to snickered, not bothering to hide her amusement.

I was speechless. Tears started to run down my face despite the fact that I was sure I would get no sympathy there. A nurse came out from a door that I had not noticed before and on seeing my state asked me what was wrong. I explained to her through my tears that I was entirely confused and lacking options. She left to get me some napkins to wipe away the damp from my face and explained to me that I could return the following Monday. She was kind, she was what a nurse was supposed to represent. Even so, I knew I would not return. I had given up. I had no business trying to raise a child; I would surely destroy myself as well as an infant.

I went back home, feeling dejected, knowing that in my mind I had already made a decision, all that was left was to get my heart on the same page. I called her would-be father and told him that we needed to have a discussion, a serious one. I was afraid to break his heart, he had gotten very excited about a daughter and I knew I would disappoint him.

He seemed to have sensed what was coming because when I told him about my intended decision he wasn't surprised. He asked me when and where. I had no answers for him. I hadn't even said the word. Abortion. I hated the word like I hated the act but was about to become the ultimate hypocrite. I was about to become a murderer and I was about to do worse than my mother had. She had spent the early years of my life abusing me both physically and emotionally. I was about to kill my own child. I was about to become a monster. I hated myself already.

That's when the dreams started, when the decision was clear in my mind. The pain also came more frequently as though she was trying to remind me that she was there. I felt suicidal for most of that time, telling myself that the world would be a brighter place without me. I prayed at first but felt blasphemous doing so. Dear Jesus please give me the strength to what... kill my child? What could I ask God for now? I knew that if I went through with this pregnancy God would help me, he would show me a way and so that made it even more evident that I was doing this for the wrong reasons. I was selfish, plain and simple, I wasn't quite ready to give up my life.

I waited until the absolute last minute to find a doctor who would perform the illegal procedure. While I waited I hoped that I would lose the baby just so that I wouldn't have to go through with it. I wished that I would die so that I wouldn't have to live with the guilt or the pain. I hoped that something would go horribly wrong with the procedure and that I would be maimed beyond repair. None of those things happened; the procedure went off without a hitch. I was in agony but I knew the physical pain would decrease. That was not the pain that I was worried about. The doctor was not unkind, nor did he judge, to him I was just a patient and he was getting paid for his services.

Two years have passed and I can barely remember the details of the procedure. I can hardly even remember the few weeks of my pregnancy. The scars on my wrists, though, serve to remind me of what happened afterward, the pain that wouldn't go away. The fungus that the antibiotics couldn't heal. I should be locked up, imprisoned like the murderer that I am but instead I walk the streets, a free woman, while people smile at me and tell others that I'm such a good person. I am not a good person. I killed my baby, my Love.

Secret love

*The ceasefire they were waiting for came. The price, however, was exorbi-*tant. Nearly fifteen hundred of their fellow, young-looking, valiant kind had moved into death like aimless night bugs rushing into the brazen headlights of a speeding vehicle. Now, blue bolts of lightning flashed erratically, tearing the black clouds into substantial parts, there, revealing the cancerous skull of the night sky. Thunder followed with wrath. The night sky was a fury of madness. The earth, in deep psychosis, heaved with pain. And the precipitation of bullets no longer fell; they no longer mixed with the weeping black sky. Amid the thick canopies of the mammoth black trees, a subtle, almost faint, childish cry of pain cropped up. It was ephemeral. In the agony of hurt, F-18 pilot, Sergeant Jason Callis awoke amid the smouldered smoking debris of the fighter jet. His body was a canvas of oil, blood, saline tears and heavenly water—Picasso gone mad. His torso pained immensely and when he did muster the strength to pull himself enough to see, he fell into a stupor. His colleague, had prudently ejected his seat, with the permission that time had allowed him; some seven minutes earlier. Callis couldn't free his seat and gripped onto the reins of the mechanical, aluminium-winged, flaming monster as his raced across the night sky. After that they were lost—in sensibility and physicality. Their bodies ceased to cooperate with their maze-like minds—a war of its own.

The rain came again. This time it was a heavy, cold, slanted sheet of shower. In its path, it tossed up the leaves of the trees violently and the cold water removed heaps of the yellow earth in its course down slope. It was this madness that woke him fully.

"Oh God, help me," he cried with the slosh of tears and raindrops running off his face.

Lightning struck, obliterating the obscurity for the fraction of a second, and, as if they were working in a partnership, the thunder followed with violence and vehemence.

"Tony," he called, the water running into his wet mouth that was soaked with blood, tears and rainwater.

But the thunder, the rain, the sway of trees drowned out all sounds. The possibility of human voices penetrating the deep jungle was impossible. For even when the thunder roared, the black, impenetrable jungle sucked the sound like a thirsty desert. He pulled himself together and bore the concentration of his pain as he hurled the sharp aluminium piece that had cut through his back and exited through his rib. The laceration bled profusely.

"Mother of God," he called, his voice a dithering call. "Help me. Please help me."

Familiar voices sang in his head. He heard his mother, a proud, persevering, old woman, praising her son as he moved pompously into battle. Behind her, he heard his sister, the silly, twenty-one-year-old Literature teacher crying, "You'll be good. God is watching over you." And when he did release his mother and hugged his sister to say goodbye, the girl shoved a small *Bible* into his dark yellow shirt pocket.

He composed himself and pulled on every sinew and tendon in his body to make sure he wasn't broken into a hundred pieces from the crash.

He would have to find Tony Rines. A good soldier never disowns his own kind. He moved through the thick, forested undergrowth among the fallen debris and decomposing twigs, leaves and dead Spanish moss. In a close corner, a deadly bushmaster watched him from the cold corners of its wicked eyes. Providence permitted him not to take the course on which the serpent lay. The snake in its cold, iniquitous manner tested the cold atmosphere with its forked, pink, worm-like tongue.

"Help," he called in the thick rain. "Somebody help me. Anybody."

Again, fate pushed him on with unseen hands and he moved through the jungle floor; a kaput satellite in the un-mapped realms of space. With the navigational will of his mind, he walked, sauntered rather, stopping every now and then, to breathe, to hug a tree, to question God about the willpower of man. It seemed to him that he had been walking for all eternity. He thought of Tony. He is alive, he heard himself saying in the theatre of his mind.

The rain abated. Now it was a light, helpless drizzle. He made out the ground. He was walking along a narrow path. But the resolve to walk was slowly ceasing his well-trained ligaments.

"God. I'm with you," he whispered in deep somnolence and pain.

He sat down on the ground. His body was beginning to play the nasty, deceitful game of failure, but his mind held out. He took out his flare gun, his only hope. And without aiming, he fired it into the night sky. The black cauldron above his head changed for a few seconds—vermilion, a bright, blaring orange, a smoky white, then black again.

Nearly twenty-five hours later he awoke to find himself lying on a stiff bed. His spasmodic eyes stared aimlessly about the white ceiling. He tried to move, at least to leap out of this sudden whiteness that had besought him, but found that his torso had grown taut as though it had been cemented in Plaster-of-Paris. Young tears grew from the corners of his eyes and trailed down his babyish, enigmatic face. He opened his mouth to call. His chest hurt, even with breathing, and, the accumulation of saliva in his mouth made talking difficult.

"Wher…" he said, staring at the cream faced, middle-aged nun clad in black as she stared into his face while she pitched a beam of yellow light in his eyes.

"Shh," she shushed him gently, "*vete a dormer* [go to sleep]."

The woman waited, stroking his thick black hair gently until he was asleep. She assessed his fine looks; put him down as a someone good, held up his hand to her heart and prayed a quiet prayer in Spanish, made the sign of the crucifix on his battered body and allowed sleep to consume his body.

Slowly he convalesced on a diet of pottage, potatoes and pineapples. The days and weeks came and all he thought about was the war. Not the war his body fought to strengthened its own defence mechanisms, but the war in which he had pledged to defend his weak country. He thought of his acquaintance, Tony Rines, lost into enemy hands; a beacon of hope snatched out of the asylum of life. He questioned himself—of where he was and what would be the outcome of this life once he recovered.

"*¿Dónde? ¿Dónde?* [Where? Where?]" he asked the nun one morning as she tended to him.

How he wished he had taken Spanish more seriously in high school.

"In God's hands," she answered in English with a philosophical prudence. "You're in God's care."

"But where am I Sister?" he besought the good sister of the unknown convent, searching her eyes.

"Saint Francine Convent for the Immaculate Conception—El Tigre."

"The enemy's hands," he whispered inaudibly. "But how come?"

"God," the middle-aged nun said, moving to the window and holding up her crucifix to her mouth, "God has a plan. *He* saved you."

He listened carefully to her. Her English was not the confirmed Standard English, but it was bent, and, some of the words seemed to take on a Spanish accent of their own.

"You did not die in the crash. The Holy Father is with you, but this is no place for a man," she said pensively, "especially one that is not of the Spanish platoon."

He thought about what the religious woman said and agreed with her, not because he was afraid of dying by the enemy's hands, but because he was afraid of dying like a runaway soldier who had deserted his kind with the hope of living.

"I must return," he said. "This is no place for me."

"You have to wait," she advised him with precedence, "the streets are crawling with the Spanish guards. People are suspicious and distrustful of everyone. Everyone believes someone is a spy, a foreigner, an intruder. You cannot—"

There was a faint, hustling shuffle on the corridor outside of the room followed by a knock on the door, then someone called in a familiar voice.

"Sister Marie, oh come quickly," the voice supplicated in Spanish.

The good sister hurried to the door and opened it. A woman of her kind entered bearing a worried look on her face.

"What is it Sister Juana?" Sister Marie asked with subdued concern.

"They're searching," she answered in Spanish, "the guards are searching everywhere."

The white-washed, terracotta convent, nearly four hundred years old, is fortified with several buried crypts and vaults and tunnels; a labyrinth in an infinite jungle.

A shout echoed in the grounds below. The good sisters realised their quandary. The guards had arrived.

"Move quickly," Sister Marie encouraged him, "you must not be caught and don't get hurt."

The sisters moved him into the closet, opened the wall behind the closet and he disappeared into the darkness with Sister Juana. Sister Marie tightened the wall and closed the closet. In the darkness, after some minutes, his eyes still couldn't adjust to the blackness. Sister Juana moved him down a narrow pathway overwhelmed with cobwebs and the mouldy smell of aged rat droppings.

In the dungeon of obscurity he remained for two days while the armed Spanish guards plagued the convent like death. He thought of the life he would have to live behind the hidden walls of the convent not knowing when his time would come. Death now was a thief in the night that could come and grab you, he thought. It could creep up inside and consume you; a disease of the mind that could control you. He hated this kind of death; death like this was miserable death.

During the shadow of a cold day, during the mid of October, Sister Marie mentioned to him that he couldn't remain in hiding forever.

"The little things give you away," she said. "Sooner or later someone will find you out. You must not let that happen—"

She stopped to think.

"It must not—not to you, not to us, and what is worst not to the Holy Father and the entire convent."

Now the sister was more practical than plaintive.

"*I* must leave," he said after studying everything that she had said.

"Yes. You must, but only when the time is right. God will tell when the time is right. In the meanwhile you have to move among them — *los guardias de español* [the Spanish guards] — fit in."

He was flummoxed: a man among nuns? Surely they won't notice, surely.

Just then Sister Juana entered the room carrying the attire of a nun, "Will this do?"

"This is fine, perfect," Sister Marie assured her.

He had fought an entire war, most cheekily; surely providence would permit him some better form of retribution than

164

to wear feminine garments, even if he had hidden in the bosoms of the enemy's pious women.

"You have to," Sister Juana coaxed him. "No one will know."

"Providence allows life and death—*you* have life," Sister Marie said, placing the black clothes on the white bed; the blackness of hell against the purity of heaven.

Now, he had no choice. They left him and moseyed out into a garden half cultivated with flaming scarlet red and chalky white ixoras and prickly citruses tall as the roof of the terracotta-roofed quadrangle. There among the other nuns, they worked, tending to a bed of young, globular melons and tall, phallus-like squashes. He studied them from a small vent and noticed how industrious they were; marching leaf-cutter ants; how busily they counted and kept meaning of their time.

He studied the garment as he dressed himself in it. Surely someone would recognise him to be a man. But as he assessed himself before the mirror, he was flabbergasted, and had to check himself bodily to make sure he hadn't evolved into a woman. He moved closer to the mirror, playing furtive facial games, certifying his realism. He was a woman now.

His days now, how leisurely and dreadfully ennui, were spent in the open courtyard and quadrangle and behind the thick, whitewashed walls, among the young, jejune nuns and the old, conservative, dour ones, doing a nun's job in tight confidentiality while moving about the grounds expertly, listlessly, hopefully tending to the overgrown fruit and vegetable garden; milking cows and picking up eggs; sweeping the worn flagstones; serving bland meals made of corn, plantain and tapioca; thinking about his frail mother and sister; reflecting on Tony; and, when time had permitted him, apart from the cyclic, timetabled Mass, he prayed with absolute ardency and hope, on tenterhooks that God, not man, would come to his rescue. He moved about bowing his head, with pretentious reverence, raising his head only when he found it absolutely necessary. He had become a nun. The determined life of piety had consumed him—he didn't feel he could live on like this, rather he knew he couldn't. At twenty-five, he shouldn't be living a celibate life, he thought. He should be free, allowed to walked among the common and eat saccharine, purple mangoes with his grandchildren during his autumnal days.

He had to find some way of moving away from this lifeless life of the convent. For when the tedious duties of the day were over, he found that solace was only found among the blossoming citrus trees. And one day, when the last of the embryonic buds had dropped, he noticed, among a patch of sunflower stalks, with big seedpods and elfin, yellow petals, he vaguely noticed, two bewildered eyes peering at him with the unfathomable vocabulary that defines love. In an instant, his heartbeat quickened. They were bright, disoriented eyes, but disappeared when they noticed that the pair had made four. He got up and the disoriented eyes, now jittery, noticed him, and quickly they moved away behind the thick citadel-like walls of the church.

New worries settled in his head. The months of mental and physical incarceration had now metastasised into a surreal tumour. He agreed that nothing was wrong with him physically, but emotionally, he felt a deep void within the arteries of his heart.

Often, he felt as though he was being watched, and even more, he was being assessed, studied, but with a different air, an air that suggested benevolence rather than malevolence.

Again he noticed the eyes—in the courtyard, at the altar, and often in the vestibule of the convent where he would answer to the call of passing mendicants while he stared out into the breadth of the world. Now the lingering, longing eyes waited on him, with hope as though they were soliciting him. This thing now was an obsession to him. The long, adoring stares; the benign, shy smiles, surely a religious woman was allowed the will to love. He had to confront her, for the sake of love; for the sake of a woman self-denied the will to love, to tell her of his flaming desires.

And after evening Mass one wet, very dark night, his chance came. The welcoming eyes were more supplicating. This time the being behind them didn't choose to rush off into illiquid space. The altar room was cleared of the pious women and the iridescent, golden flames from the candles threw monstrous shadows on the cold, white, but now yellow walls.

He walked up to her. She moved to the window with an air of censored anxiety while she adjusted the hood of her clothes.

"Who are you?" he implored. "I cannot bear to see this shy smile upon your sweet face."

He moved closer to her. She nodded her head, as if to ensure conformity.

"My heart beats with love, but more with fear," he said, his voice a wavering one. "Please tell, who *are* you?"

He sought courage, and put his hand on her shoulder so she would turn to look him in his eyes. Her heart beat quickened, and his was racing with vehemence. He knew of the implications that were before him, for his undertaking was equal to the gruesome war that he fought, but he hadn't thought of the consequences. The beat of his heart was now a rhythmic *patump patump* in his ears; his unblinking, depthless, black eyes were filled with angst, yet they seemed so tranquil behind the restless melancholy of his thin face.

She moved away; a baby's step, as if encouraging him to follow, to solicit a more sturdy inquiry. He followed.

A light drizzle was penetrating the darkness outside.

"Who are you?" he supplicated.

She turned around with alacrity; her eyes gaping over him in a squint. He grew worried for a moment.

She smiled.

"*Bonita* [beautiful]," she laughed.

"*¿Quien tu erts?* [Who are you?]" he questioned. His face had grown into an enigmatic map.

"*Mi amor* [My love]," she chuckled, her voice now becoming mannish.

He was dumbfounded. His eyes widened with the riddle.

"*Mi amor*—my love—my love," the woman joked as she removed her hood.

"Tony!" he shouted in surprise. "You dog, you're alive! Alive!"

They threw themselves into each other's arms and embraced tightly.

"Yes my friend. I'm alive, I'm alive."

Lightning struck. The wind blew. The flames died. The room grew dark. The rain returned.

Raymond Yusuf

Raymond Yusuf is the author of *The Only Man* and *Secret love*. He teaches grade ten and eleven English, and resides in the small countryside village of Supply, Guyana. He hopes to pursue a fulltime career as a writer, poet and novelist. Apart from reading and painting, he spends his free time writing at the beach, in a bus or under a tree. He has completed three collections of poems: *Crimes of Love*, *100 Sonnets of Love* and *Melancholy of Love*. Presently he is working on a collection: *Dreaming of Tigers*. He is inspired by the poetry of Yevtushenko, Whitman, Neruda, Tagore, Milosz and Heaney.

Schaunne Badloo

Schaunne Badloo is the author of *The Jumbie Boy*. Born in 1974, Balmain Village, Couva, the heart of Central Trinidad, he is the first of the five children of Kenneth and Kamala Badloo. Although his career is in finance, he has always reserved a place in his heart for local folktales of the "Lagahoo" and the "Soucouyant" told by his grandmother and other elders in his family; these stories, mixed with actual events, left an indelible fondness for the "Jumbie encounter stories" of old. On finding out about the competition, he set out to create a narrative that would embody modern day excitement with that of an "old time" scare. He hopes his account leaves the reader with the same satisfied smile of nostalgia and intrigue that he felt while writing. He is quite honoured to have a place among such talented writers and to be part of such a great undertaking which he feels certain will become a milestone in Caribbean publishing and hopefully ignite the author in every reader. *The Jumbie Boy* is dedicated to his little sister Kimberly.

The Jumbie Boy, page 11

Nathifa Swan

Nathifa Swan is the author of *Accepted*. She is from Trinidad and Tobago and has enjoyed reading and writing for as long as she could remember. She is extremely fond of poetry. Currently, she is furthering her education at Point Fortin East Secondary and would love to become a famous author or chef when she leaves school.

Accepted, page 21

Victor Peter-George

Victor Peter-George is the author of *Crazy Mary*. He was born in 1960, Point Fortin, Trinidad, where his love for reading and writing flourished, and recalls memories of his parents reading bedtime stories to him and his siblings. In secondary school his exposure to West Indian literature whetted his appetite and during this time his father encouraged him to read two novels per week. He is the author of many poems and short stories and most recently completed the manuscript for his first novel, *Mango Mouth*.

Crazy Mary, page 31

Joseph Bridglal

Joseph Bridglal is the author of *The muddy shoes*. He was born in 1965, resides in Woodland, Trinidad, attended Naparima College and currently works as a Quality Assurance Supervisor in a steel manufacturing plant. Jane Eyre is his favourite author and he began writing short stories in 2010. *The muddy shoes* is his first story submitted for publication.

The muddy shoes, page 40

Samantha Salandy

Samantha Salandy is the author of *Lovingly mischievous*. She was born in 1990 and after she discovered books, she read anything she could get her hands on. She loves how writing could take someone to a place *she* created and the impact it could have on people.

In secondary school her love for writing and The Arts increased. She and other peers who shared the same zeal founded *The Writer's Club*. Later on, she became the editor of the school newspaper at the Corpus Christi College, which taught her how challenging writing could be, and although the newspaper wasn't a big event in the school's history, for her it was and still is. She's currently pursuing an advanced diploma in business management.

Lovingly mischievous, page 50

Sandra Sealy

Sandra Sealy is the author of *Big rock soup*. She is an award-winning freelance writer/editor of poetry, short stories, plays, corporate material and articles, as well as an arts tutor and spoken-word artist. This creative mother and wife's work has been widely published in the region and beyond in several publications like *POUI* (UWI Barbados), *SHE Caribbean Magazine* (St. Lucia), *Isla Firme* (Venezuela), *Calabash: A Caribbean Journal of Arts & Letters* (NYU, USA) and *St. Somewhere Journal* (cyberspace). Her poem *Beauty Of The Bald Head* (1998), moved from page to stage in 2005, as a critically acclaimed CD spoken-word jazz single, to a music video premiering at the African & Caribbean Film Festival (Pelican Films).

As a stalwart in Barbados' literary arena, she has co-ordinated many arts events and adjudicated literary competitions and poetry slams-even at a national level like the National Independence Festival of Creative Arts (NIFCA) as a Literary Arts Judge. This Anansesem.com Editor also created Seawoman's Caribbean Writing Opps *(www.seawoman.wordpress.com)*, which enjoys a high Google ranking.

Big rock soup, page 61

Angelia Lallan

Angelia Lallan is the author of *Under the poui*. Her love for reading inspires her to write because her pen expresses who she is, her dreams, ideas, imagination and personal life. She is a devout Hindu and describes her fiancé as a rock solid support in everything she does and enjoys, including badminton, karaoke, music and spending time with loved ones. She is currently working and furthering her studies in accounting and information systems and hopes to be a published author.

Under the poui, page 71

Lisa-Anne Julien

Lisa-Anne Julien is the author of *God Save the Queen*. She was born in Trinidad. In 1992 she was awarded a scholarship to study dance in Guadeloupe and within a year of being there she won another to attend the Alvin Ailey American Dance Centre in New York. She also attended the Martha Graham School for Contemporary Dance for one year. After three years in New York, Lisa-Anne began to feel the life of the starving artist was highly overrated and so left for London in 1996. Wanting her life to make bolder social statements she completed an Undergraduate Degree in Development Studies and a Masters Degree in Social Policy from the London School of Economics. In order to pay her tuition, she worked as a nursing assistant in a psychiatric hospital for four years and was humbled by having to witness the fragility of the human mind and body.

In 2002, Lisa-Anne moved to South Africa and has since worked as a researcher, writer and consultant in the field of gender and women's rights and HIV and AIDS. As a freelance writer she has written for magazines such as *'O', The Oprah Magazine South Africa, Elle South Africa, Psychologies South Africa, SHE Caribbean, The New African*, local newspapers and peer-reviewed journals such as *Agenda Feminist Journal*. In May 2008 Lisa-Anne was one of ten finalists for the Women & Home Magazine South Africa Short Story Competition. In November 2008 she was selected as a winner in the "Highly Commended" category of the Commonwealth Short Story Competition. In October 2010 Lisa-Anne's first book, a romance novel set in a South African township, was published by Nollybooks. She currently lives in Johannesburg with her two beautiful children.

God Save the Queen, page 82

Nikita Mungal

Nikita Mungal is the author of *The Winged Girl*. At twenty four, she is the dedicated mother of one and is currently pursuing her Bachelors of Education at the University of Trinidad and Tobago. Along with writing, her most pleasurable activities include spending time with family, karate, movies, reading, indulging in The Arts and socialising with friends. Her philosophy is respecting others "regardless of…," never giving up, valuing life and having fun on a daily basis. She sees herself as driven, focussed and committed to reaching her fullest potential and has great aspirations of being an influential person and writer.

The Winged Girl, page 92

Merisa Roberts

Merisa Roberts is the author of *Village story*. She enjoys writing fiction, drama and poetry, and the works of Sarah Dessen, Meg Cabot, Louisa May Alcott, Cornelia Funke, Scott Westerfield.

Village story, page 102

Arlene Walrond

Arlene Walrond is the author of *Tears for my mother*. She was born and raised in Sainte Madeleine, a village in south Trinidad. In 2004, *Caribbean Compass* published one of her articles. Since then she has completed a novel and is midway through the second. One of her poems was selected for the *2010 Animal Antics Anthology* in Britain.

Tears for my mother, page 112

Andrea Wilson

Andrea Wilson is the author of *When we were alone*. She was born on April 20, 1974, in the small town of Linden, Guyana. Situated sixty-five miles up the Demerara River, Linden is known primarily as a bauxite mining town. At an early age her love for and fascination with reading was stimulated by a dad whose Louis L'Amour books littered their home and for whom she waited eagerly at the end of each day for the tales that he spun about wars, cowboys and many, many heroes. Her respect for the profundity and power of words was instilled by a grandfather who too soon went blind, making her his reading 'eyes'. She would spend many hours reading aloud for him the news and other select books and was never allowed to skip 'the big words'.

She was always considered a promising student at the Mackenzie High School where she participated in debates and was selected Head Prefect. Her career as a teacher started soon after her graduation and during her early years in the secondary system she was able to further develop her passion for The Arts through teaching Literature and encouraging student participation in the Performing Arts. She obtained her professional qualifications for teaching English at the secondary level in the year 2000 and was awarded the best graduating student prize for Region Ten along with the best graduating English and Education student. She then pursued the Bachelor of Education programme in English and Humanities Studies at the University of Guyana and graduated Valedictorian, winning the President's Medal along with the Teachers' Union Award, Eusi Kwayana and Canadian Guild Award.

When we were alone, page 122

Tara Ramsingh

Tara Ramsingh is the author of *The beach awaits*. She was born in Princes Town, Trinidad, and currently lives in Rio Claro with her family. Her story was inspired by actual events with certain twists. Her ultimate goal is to feature on a best sellers list.

The beach awaits, page 130

Sadé Collins

Sadé Collins is the author of *Dis anime ting again*. She is an animation student at the University of Trinidad and Tobago and lives in Belmont, Trinidad and Tobago, with her family. She took up writing when she was six years old. Originally developed as a school assignment, *Dis anime ting again* was inspired by her deep love for the Japanese animation franchise known as anime. Like many Trinbagonian teens, she is an anime otaku – a Japanese term that describes people who are obsessed with anime. She dreams of one day turning her ideas into colourfully innovative animations as popular as anime.

Dis anime ting again, page 139

Kalifa Clyne

Kalifa Clyne is the author of *Troubles bourne*. She is a young Trinidadian journalist at Guardian Media Limited with a passion for storytelling and writing as an art form. She is a poet and aspiring novelist who lives for the written word.

Troubles bourne, page 150

CPSIA information can be obtained at www.ICGtesting.com
Printed in the USA
LVOW130546210812

295225LV00002B/2/P